# Space Orcs Volume 4

## The Last of the Orcqlaneasions

Solar Black

Solar Blackboard Publishing

The characters and events portrayed in this book are fictitious. Any similarity to real persons, living or dead, is coincidental and not intended by the author.



ISBN: 979-8-9926933-4-8

Cover design by: Kollage Graphics

For permissions, inquiries, or more information, visit: www.solarblackboard.com

Printed in the United States of America.

# Contents

# DEDICATION

For the three great loves of my life:
Frank, my first love;
Michael, the love that was supposed to last a lifetime;
and Tony, on again, off again, mostly off.

SOLAR BLACK

# SPACE ORCS AND THE JUDGE

## THE LAST OF THE ORCQLANEASIONS

# SPACE ORCS AND THE JUDGE

## THE LAST OF THE ORCQLANEASIONS

# CHAPTER 1: Judith Jimenez-Jackson

What if the fairytales had it all wrong? What if there wasn't really an evil stepmother, but instead vicious, awful stepchildren. Their sole mission being to bring years of misery into your life for committing the cardinal sin of loving their father. If I wrote a fairytale, that's how I'd tell the story with the stepmother being the victim, not the villain. But even as I thought about it, I realized, who was I kidding? I could never cast myself in the role of victim, especially at the hands of my miserable stepsons.

"J.J. Come to the conference room, we've got a case for you. Now!"

And right on cue, a deep voice so hauntingly similar to my late husband's demanded my presence for what was sure to be another petty assignment for nothing more than a shoplifting or vagrancy case.

Although now that tougher laws had been passed in the latest zero tolerance administration, vagrancy had become a much more serious offense.

As I gathered my tablet and made my way to the conference room, the last visible location of my husband's presence in the law firm we created, I thought about my most recent vagrancy case.

The young woman involved had received a reprieve when our new mysterious alien client arranged for her employment in one of their holdings on the moon.

Remembering her elation at finding out she was not going to a work camp for a minimum four-year stint, but was instead traveling to manage a lunar salon in space, was almost contagious.

It was the closest I had been to even a semblance of joy. Even though I was happy for her, I couldn't shake the pall of grief that had encased my heart these last two years without the presence of my best friend, my husband, and the father to my obnoxious stepchildren.

I walked with measured steps into the conference room, unsure of what fresh hell my stepsons had in store for me today.

"It took you long enough. This is an urgent matter, and you're just dragging your damn feet."

"Good morning, Jason, Stephen." I gave my usual greeting, not so much because I wanted to, but to deflect the open hostility bouncing off each of them.

Looking past them, I took in my favorite thing about the conference room: the wall size lithograph of *El Velorio* by Francisco Oller. I had shown my late husband, William, the painting housed in Puerto Rico's Museum of Art and Anthropology during our first trip together to the island. He'd been insistent on getting permission from my stern great-grandmother, Abuela, before announcing our engagement.

The painting always brought me back to the nostalgia of that moment, when I was young and in love, in defiance of everything and everyone around me. If only I'd known what the future held, perhaps I would have made different decisions. But then again, maybe not.

"J.J. Are you listening? They've specifically requested you, not the firm, only you," Stephen said, irritated.

Truthfully, I hadn't been listening, musing about roads not taken and the like. *El pasado se queda donde está.* There was no point pretending I'd heard anything, and it was much better to just move forward in the moment.

"Who has requested me for what case?" I said evenly, not letting my irritation show at being summoned like a first year associate rather than a founding partner.

"That alien client you brought in, MDS Intergalactic. Apparently, they're in some hot water and have requested a hearing with the Galactic Alliance. They're insisting on meeting with you as soon as possible," Jason said.

"You want me to take a meeting with a client off-planet? Absolutely not," I said adamantly.

"That's not the right answer, J.J. We've already reassigned your cases to other associates and cleared your schedule. They want you there right away," Stephen, the more hostile of the two, said.

"I'm not going to God knows where because some aliens requested it. I'm not some desperate young woman with no other options," I said. My mind flashed again to images of my vagrancy client, Sunni Davis, her smile a mix of desperation and gratitude.

"Everything's already been paid, and the contract is secured. You leave for Nyokaa at the end of the week," Jason added.

"Nyokaa? I don't even know what or where that is. Why wouldn't I be going to the Galactic Alliance Conclave?" I was curious about this new venue, despite the fact that I had absolutely no intention of going anywhere.

"Your clients have sought asylum on Nyokaa, and that is your first stop before the hearing is scheduled before the GA Conclave," Jason added.

"I'm not going," I said definitively.

"Fine, then you can pay us back for breaking the contract," Stephen said before sliding an abbreviated financial agreement in front of me.

I was astounded at the amount of money the clients were offering. There was no way I could pay that amount, even if I liquidated all my assets, which was probably exactly what my stepsons wanted me to do anyway.

"I need to think about this." Even as I said the words, I knew what my decision would be.

"You have until tomorrow morning," Stephen said with a sneer.

I left the conference room shaken. It was so uncanny hearing the same timbre of my beloved's voice coming from his heinous offspring. Neither of William's children had ever liked me, due in no small part to their mother, Kim, who constantly referred to me as, "that Spanish nigga bitch."

There was no changing the past. And even if I could, I don't know that I would.

I just wished I had more time with William. His final days were emblazoned in my heart and mind as the memories of our last night together came into sharp focus.

***

*"Mi amor, what are you doing out of bed? You should have called me if you needed something," I said worriedly.*

*"I'm good, baby." William's smooth voice was now gone, having been ravaged by cancer that had spread from his lungs to his throat and, more recently, his brain.*

*He shuffled over to the sofa, his strong six-foot-two frame slumped from both age and disease.*

*"Come sit with me, baby. We need to talk," he said.*

*I was flustered seeing him out of his bed and in the living room. I'd had our bedroom refitted with a medical bed, monitor, and all the equipment necessary for him to stay home rather than enter hospice. Witnessing him out of it and on the living room sofa was nothing short of miraculous.*

*He patted the cushion next to him and I went to sit beside him, hugging him gently, waiting for him to begin whatever had compelled him from his deathbed.*

*"I'm sorry, babygirl, for all the shit I put you through," he said, and I put my fingers to his lips and shook my head.*

*I didn't want his last words to me to be about regret and mistakes, but he pulled my hand away.*

*"I gotta say this, baby. This is my last chance. I lied so much, hurt so many people, but I wanted you so bad," he said slowly.*

*I didn't want to listen, but I forced myself to, even though I knew where it was headed.*

*"I should have told you I was married when we got together, but I was so unhappy. And you—you were like a breath of fresh air." He paused, as if the words hurt to come out.*

*"I'd never seen a more beautiful woman before or since. The way you hung onto my every word. The curious light in your honey brown eyes. I knew it was wrong to fall for my student, but I was lost the moment*

*you stepped into my lecture hall." His voice caught again, either from the words or the pain of speaking. I tried to get him to stop, but he would not allow it. He was determined for me to hear his words.*

*"I regret how everything went down with Kim and the boys. She poisoned them against you from the start, and nothing I've done has ever redeemed me in their eyes." He took a halting breath and continued.*

*"I blamed you for my relationship with my sons, but I should have worked harder." The sorrow in the words he spoke was clearly visible in the etched lines of his hollowed face.*

*"So instead of being a better father, I became a worse husband," he said, as if the words were wrenched from his body.*

*"William, it's all in the past, my love. Don't trouble your thoughts with this. We made it through the rocky parts, stronger than ever," I said, hoping to steer his mind away from its present course. He shook his head, unmoved from the path he had set for himself.*

*"I'm sorry, baby, for fucking around. You didn't deserve that. I caused you a lifetime of pain, when you are the love of my life," he said in tears.*

*It was hard hearing this from the man I loved with all my heart. The first time I realized he had cheated was after my third miscarriage. I blamed myself. I felt like it was my fault for not being able to give him a family, after he had left his family to be with me.*

*As much as I loved him, it hurt knowing that I wasn't enough for him. I tried to distance myself from him. We'd even gone through trial separations, but we always got back together.*

*After my fifth miscarriage, we stopped trying for a baby altogether. We lived separate lives but stayed together, building our law firm and making a name for ourselves in the legal community.*

*I focused on my career and earned a seat on the federal bench before my fortieth birthday. When the planet got smaller with the acknowl-*

*edgment that we were not alone in the universe, I was appointed to the World Court as a magistrate judge.*

*William continued to grow the law firm we started together, eventually bringing in both his sons after they graduated with their law degrees.*

*We settled into a comfortable routine. I still loved him, but it wasn't the passionate, all-consuming love it had been before. He had been my law professor, mentor, lover, husband, and finally, in the end, my best friend. He wasn't a bad man, just a flawed one.*

*For my part, I hadn't made the right decisions either. I should never have started an affair with a married man with children, but I was young and impulsive. Our decision to be together not only caused a rift in his family, it caused one in mine, as well. My family never truly accepted my relationship with William, and sensing their reticence, I spent less and less time with them and more time establishing my career.*

*It wasn't the life I had expected, but it was a good life, at least until William's cancer diagnosis. The disease was fast and fluid, leaving him a shell of the dynamic man he had been. I gave up my judicial appointment to take care of William full-time.*

*We'd been together almost thirty years. There was a lot of pain and hurt between us, but I refused to let him take that with him to the grave.*

*"Mi amor, I love you with all my heart, body, and soul, and there is nothing I would change in my life with you. With love, there's no need for forgiveness," I said, hugging his frail body close to mine.*

*I helped him get back to his bed, and he held my hand as he went to sleep. He seemed at peace, and perhaps he finally was. He passed away quietly that night, the cancer finally overtaking his body.*

***

With a fresh perspective due in no small part to my memories of William, the next morning I came into work ready to tell my stepsons my decision. I went into my office and saw that all my personal belongings had been boxed up.

Those two had a lot of nerve. I went in search of the brothers to give them a piece of my mind, and what I saw caused me to pause. Someone was ripping down the beautiful lithograph that William had commissioned. I put my hand on the glass door handle to go in and halt whoever it was, but stopped in my tracks. The vandal turned to face me with venom in her eyes. It was Kim, William's first wife and Jason and Stephen's mother.

She was ready for a fight, but I was too old, too heartsick, and too tired to give her one.

I went back to my office, gathered my belongings, and left.

# CHAPTER 2: Elder Helvich Dralvion - Space Orc

"Where is Nerisch?" I asked my bound brother Coervich.

"Probably in the Exercise Bay, most likely re-enacting battles from a Distant Wars holodisc," he replied.

"He goes there every day. It would not hurt him to prepare for our new assignment at the Galactic Alliance. This is not like Quadrant Three. This new role puts us in the center of the universe, so to speak, at least in terms of diplomacy," I said, exasperated.

"I think he feels like he learned all he needed to know from our predecessors: Orenik Cyradis, Maerik Valtorin, Auerik Zephiron," Coervich said.

I sighed. My bound brother Nerisch was least suited of any Orc-qlaneasion to be an Elder. Even though it was expected that warriors who survived until their hair was white would assume their duties in the Directorate of Orcqlaneasus, Nerisch quietly defied the conventions.

Of course, he would befriend Elders with a human mate and several hybrid sons. All of Orcqlaneasus had learned of Elder Orenik's defiance to Chief Elder Illbrien when faced with sanctions against his mate Earth Mother Vivien Johnson. Many believed that Orenik would be a better choice to lead Orcqlaneasus, especially as we entered this new age of hope for a future with children and mates. So far, twenty-five of our brethren had found mates and sired more than fifty hybrid children.

Rather than getting debriefs from the former ambassadors, he spent his time with them tutoring the small hybrids on rudimentary forms of combat, although due to the age and disposition of the children, it was more play than actual competitive form.

For my part, I was conflicted by the arrival of the so-called saviors, "Earth Mothers" as they had been deemed. When I first encountered them during a convocation of families called by Chief Elder Illbrien, I, like every other Orcqlaneasion male, was struck by their beauty. But much like my warrior brother Qorath Dral, I found the humans' influence on their Orcqlaneasion mates troubling.

Coervich, who had always been stoic, offered no indication of his thoughts. Our bond yielded nothing I could interpret. That was not unusual, but it left me with no position to weigh against my own.

Nerisch was clearer. His fascination with the Earth Mothers was evident. The distant hope of claiming a mate and beginning a family had affected him like a draught of Praxiumn elixir: sweet, heady, and disorienting.

We were not aligned. Neither of my brethren shared my thoughts, and that in itself was unsettling. I would keep my observations to myself. Perhaps our new assignment to the Galactic Alliance General

Assembly would offer insight into the motives and machinations of these human beings.

"Helvich, check the comms. We are getting a call," Coervich said.

In my musings, I had not noticed the incoming signal from the Directorate of Orcqlaneasus, specifically from the call sign of our Chief Elder Illbrien Rezz. Before answering the call, I sent a disruptive message to Nerisch, alerting him to come to the bridge.

Always quick, Nerisch entered the bridge after I initiated greetings with the Chief Elder.

Elder Illbrien saw Nerisch enter and began his discourse.

"I am glad that you are assembled together. I have received a troubling message that needs to be handled delicately and immediately."

"It seems our pesky little nemesis, the Pstoadys scientists that we have been looking for, have requested a mediation hearing to be held at the Galactic Alliance Conclave."

Coervich responded to the news. "That is good news, then. We have been trying to bring them to heel for quite a while."

"No, under no circumstances can we allow this to happen," Elder Illbrien responded vehemently.

"I do not understand, Chief Elder. I concur with my bound brother. We expended a great amount of time and resources to capture the elusive Pstoadys, only for them to be granted asylum in Nyokaa. This finally brings them within reach," I countered.

"As you know, we are rebuilding our society, one family at a time. It is no secret that our people are nearly extinct, and our planet rich in resources has been seen as ripened fruit ready to be plucked. For this reason, we have closed our borders to all outsiders, except for the human females that we have mated and who have borne our sons. Now that re-population is possible, our survival is still at risk. No one must know about the secret of the Pstoadys' experimentation on both the humans and Orcqlaneasions. We now have young sons, none older than five annums, and their mothers, our mates, that we must protect as much as, or even more than, our beloved planet."

"We understand, Chief Elder, and will follow your direction. How shall we proceed?" said Nerisch.

His quick response surprised both Coervich and me, since he generally showed very little interest in the political intrigues attached to being a diplomat.

"I have instituted a stealth all-call alert, notifying Orcqlaneasions in each sector to return to the homeworld," the Chief Elder stated.

"Since you have several contacts from your diplomatic assignment in Quadrant Three, you should return there and contact the Pstoadys through the Nyoka monarchy. The Nyoka are trusted allies, and any mediation should take place there, not in the Galactic Assembly," Elder Illbrien proclaimed.

I found no holes in Chief Elder Illbrien's logic. It was a solid plan. In recent months, his choice as leader had been brought into question, but his strategic resolve in handling this tricky situation, while maintaining the security of Orcqlaneasus and its residents, assured me of his sound capability.

"We will change course to Nyokaa, and keep you apprised of our progress with the Pstoady mediation," I said to the Elder before ending the transmission.

Immediately, Nerisch went to his station at the automated navigation console and input our new destination. I looked over at him and could see his glee in returning to our former diplomatic site.

In the years we spent in Nyokaa, Nerisch had excelled in making alliances within the Nyokan royal court. He was a good friend to Dukari Asani and their mate Lady Kayla, and a trusted mentor of their elder sons Kamari and Kajari Asani.

"It will be good to return to Quadrant Three once again, brothers," Nerisch said happily.

"I agree, brother. I fear that I have been away from our homeworld so long that I struggle to find my place in it again. Especially now, with the advent of the younglings ever present," Coervich said. "Never have I felt the weight of my white hair more than around their youthful exuberance."

Nerisch burst into laughter at Coervich's words, and I struggled to maintain a smile. The hybrid sons were extremely rambunctious, and being in close confines with them took up energy reserves maintained for rigorous training in preparation for battle.

It was good that the younglings had a cadre of sires too, since their energy was boundless.

"Brother, you have gotten too set in your ways. The younglings are a joy to be around, especially the elder-kind. I enjoyed my time teaching them to spar and defensive claw combat. They will make mighty warriors some day," Nerisch said, recounting his recent time on Orcqlaneasus.

"Yes, but they must also learn discipline, which so far seems to be sorely lacking. Even the elder-kind of the Chief Elder and his brethren are little terrors, although given their sires, that is not unexpected," Coervich said, exasperated.

This time, I could not contain my mirth, joining my brother Nerisch in hearty laughter at my brother's expense.

Good-natured as always, Coervich reflected on his words and joined us in laughter as we pursued our new mission to our old station in Quadrant Three.

***

The destination to Quadrant Three was expected to take far less time, due in no small part to the upgrade we received as the official diplomatic envoys from Orcqlaneasus to Quadrant Four. We had been granted a new diplomatic spacecraft, which far exceeded our previous vessel in many ways. This one was more spacious, more luxurious, and much more in keeping with the trappings of chief diplomats of the Galactic Alliance.

Luxury notwithstanding, the ship was also faster and more agile, despite its size and ostentatiousness. It was equipped with advanced artificial intelligence, capable of long-range navigation, secure diplomatic transmissions, stealth operations, and a ready arsenal of both short- and long-range defensive weaponry.

Our old ship had been battle tested, having survived multiple engagements during the Distant Wars. This vessel, though not without defenses, had been built for diplomacy. It was a ship of peace, not war.

Traveling at Galactic Standard, we reached Nyokaa space in two weeks, half the time it would have taken aboard our previous vessel.

We were greeted by the security drones that encircled the planet, broadcasting a universal message to all travelers. Using our diplomatic credentials, we circumvented the normal bureaucracy and contacted our Nyokan friends, the Dukari twins.

It had admittedly been a curiosity to us upon first meeting the twin Dukaris to learn that they shared one name and, for most of their lives, had shared a single identity. It was not until they had found a lifemate, Kayla, a human female, that they were permitted to exist openly as two individual beings instead of sharing a life as one.

It was an unusual occurrence, but then all species had their peculiarities. As an Elder of Orcqlaneasus, one of the last of a thousand of our kind, my brethren and I were in no position to render judgment on any other beings.

The comms alerted us to an incoming transmission, and the twin visages of Dukari materialized on the vid screen.

"Greetings, old friends. What brings you back to Quadrant Three? When you left us for the brighter stars of Quadrant Four, we assumed you wouldn't be returning, at least not so soon," Dukari[1] said.

"Perhaps they missed the vibrancy of Nyokaa over the staid halls of the Galactic Alliance," Dukari[2] said.

Nerisch immediately strode forth and responded to his Nyokan friends. "We were looking forward to the quiet of the General Assembly after years navigating the intrigues of the Nyokan royal court. How fares your Scion? Still wielding power with the precision of a Trilium Blade?" Nerisch asked good-humoredly.

"She fares well, ceding more authority to her appointed heirs, though not enough to make a difference in her rule, but just enough to make it a hardship to manage them," Dukari[1] said, exasperated.

"Their mother is at her wit's end, with both the Scion and her interference in our sons' lives," Dukari[2] said. "I much preferred when our aunt had a very claws-off approach, as she did with my brother and me. Naming Kajari and Kamari as her ascendant heirs has been problematic."

Seeing that these old friends would speak at length about domestic issues, I levied my own request.

"We are here on a diplomatic mission. It seems you have given asylum to two Pstoady scientists that wrought a series of problems to Orcqlaneasus."

"Ah, you speak of Torvak and Tovak," Dukari[1] said.

"They are quite in demand. This is the second request we have had this day to meet with them," Dukari[2] said.

"Second request to meet with the Pstoadys? Who else has interest in the refugees?" Coervich asked.

"They have retained legal counsel from Earth. Their attorney should be meeting with them as we speak," Dukari$^1$ said.

"Human? Their counsel is from Earth? Is their counsel a human female, possibly with brown skin like your mate's Kayla?"

"Yes, she is a human female, but her hue is not nearly the same as our Kayla. Although it is somewhat similar to our children's in human form, perhaps a shade lighter," Dukari$^1$ said.

"Why does that matter?" Dukari$^2$ said.

"Stop the meeting. She cannot meet with the Pstoadys," Coervich demanded.

"Explain this," Dukari$^2$, the less peaceful twin, demanded.

"We will explain all, but not over comms," Nerisch said.

"Detain or quarantine the human, but under no circumstances should she be allowed near the Pstoadys," I said. "We will take a shuttle and meet you in your quarters to explain in person."

# CHAPTER 3: Sorry Ms. Jackson

Snakes. Why'd it have to be snakes?

Yeah, I know I sounded like a line from a famous movie, but it was all I could do not to scream hysterically when I saw actual life-size snake people.

In my rush to get inoculated for space sickness, chipped with a translation device, and read up on galactic case law, I completely forgot to research the people of Nyokaa.

¡Puñeta!

I mean, I understood that their species was reptilian, but somehow the reality of what that meant didn't quite compute in my brain.

To be fair, the Nyokans gave me lovely accommodations and had been extremely hospitable, but I just couldn't get past the whole snake thing. Shaking off my instinctual revulsion, I tried to relax in the room or living pod I'd been assigned. But here again, I found the foreignness disconcerting. There were no chairs, just overstuffed beanbag-like things strewn throughout the space. The design looked like a mix of Asian fusion and boho chic in a strange, alien combination.

I paced the room for a while, working through nervous energy. I sat for a bit in one of the beanbags and tried to work on my tablet, but it was too uncomfortable without any support for my back. Damn, getting old was a bitch. In frustration, I started pacing again, hoping to collect my thoughts.

When I first arrived, I was under the impression that I would be taken to see my clients immediately, so the delay was unsettling. I needed to confer with my clients, set up a meeting with the Space Orc representatives, and get the whole thing over with as soon as possible, and get back to my life, such that it was.

I wasn't sure what awaited me at home, except an empty house I'd once shared with William, one his nefarious sons were trying desperately to steal right out from under me. I couldn't go back to the law firm either, especially after seeing Kim heartlessly rip down the last remaining vestige of William from the office.

Thoughts of a bleak future combined with the effects of interstellar travel finally collided. I sank back into the beanbag and tried to rest. It must have worked, because the next thing I knew, I was sound asleep.

***

The twinkling of chimes woke me from my much-needed rest. I looked around and saw through the glass windows that it was now nighttime. Looking out at the scenic view, I was struck by the beauty of the alien landscape.

The capital city, or crown city, was a futuristic marvel. A multitude of soft, bright lights shimmered in a myriad of colors. I stood transfixed, gazing at the skyline, but was interrupted again by the chimes that had first awakened me.

I felt ridiculous realizing I didn't know how to answer the chimes or stop them outright. I was a complete *jíbara* in this environment.

Cautiously, I walked to the sliding doors I had entered through earlier, hoping there would be some kind of mechanism to silence the sound without alerting any of the snake people to my distress.

I placed my hand on the door and it slid open. This time, I wasn't greeted by snakes, but by gigantic, seven- or eight-foot-tall, white-haired Space Orcs. As intimidating as they were in person, I had at least seen them before in vid clips during the Distant Wars. The ones in the footage had been younger, with long black hair and body armor. These were older but still formidable. They wore long white robes, ceremonial from the look of them, embroidered with gold stitching in a pattern I didn't recognize.

"Greetings, Earth counselor. May we enter and speak with you regarding the matter you are here to attend? I am Elder Helvich Dralvion, and these are my bound brothers, Elders Nerisch Braedaris and Coervich Thaloryn."

I stood there gaping and could only nod. I stepped aside so they could enter.

I knew I was staring, but I couldn't help it. I had always been attracted to tall, ultra-masculine men like William. And despite their alien features, including pointed ears, green skin, and thick, waist-length white hair, they were beautiful. They were like green mythical gods come to life. *¡Ave María purísima!*

I composed myself and found my voice. "I'm J.J. Jackson. I'm glad you're here so we can meet, but I have to let you know I haven't spoken with my clients yet. I'm not sure what we can accomplish until I do."

I leaned into my years as a professional jurist to steady myself. I had read the request from my clients. They had sought asylum on Nyokaa for some wrong or crime committed against the Orcqlaneasion people. The exact offense wasn't stated in detail, so I was hoping to get the information from the Space Orcs themselves.

The one introduced as Elder Coervich spoke. "That is why we have come, despite the late hour. You cannot meet with the Pstoadys."

"What do you mean? I came here to meet them, to represent them. Why can't I meet them? Has something happened?" My mind raced with a million possibilities.

Elder Helvich stepped forward, his voice firm with unspoken command. "It would be too dangerous for you to be in contact with the Pstoadys. We cannot allow it."

"You have no authority to stop me from meeting with my clients. They are the sole reason I'm here." The irritation in my voice was growing faster than I could check it.

"In addition to our role as Elders of the Directorate, the Orcqlaneasions' primary edict is to serve as peacekeepers throughout the galaxy," Helvich said, his tone imperious. "It is under that edict that we have determined you will not meet with the Pstoady scientists, Torvak and Tovak."

They turned toward the door as if the matter were settled. As if I hadn't spoken at all.

"Wait a minute. That's it? I can't meet with my clients, and we're done? What happens next?"

Helvich answered without looking back. "We will petition the Nyokans to release the Pstoadys into our custody, ending their claim of asylum. We will transport them back to Orcqlaneasus, where they will answer for their crimes."

"You can't do that. They asked for impartial mediation between both parties to avoid exactly what you're talking about," I said, defending clients I hadn't even seen.

The only one who had not yet spoken, Elder Nerisch, stepped forward and positioned himself directly in front of me. He had to be at least two feet taller than me, with broad shoulders, and thick white braids that hung past his waist. Up close, I caught his scent; it felt familiar, but I couldn't place it. It stirred something in me I didn't have time to examine.

"It would not be safe for you to meet the Pstoadys," he said. His voice was a deep, rich baritone that resonated deep within me. "So, we cannot allow it."

I had always been a sucker for deep voices. This one didn't just sound good, it felt good. In another situation, I might have leaned in and let it wrap itself around me. But I was too angry at the high-handed way they had handled me.

"I will petition the Nyokans to deny your request and allow the Pstoadys to remain free of your custody," I said. My voice was steady, even though my heart skipped a beat.

Nerisch looked down at me and smiled. I caught a glimpse of fangs, just enough to remind me that whatever charm he carried, this was still an alien creature.

"You can try."

And just like that, they walked out of the room through the sliding doors.

I stood there wondering what had just happened. I had been managed quite effectively, and now I was at a loss as to what to do next. Still, I knew I had to do something. I had to act.

I wasn't sure of the time, and the snake person who had escorted me here hadn't returned to check on me or offer assistance.

I would have to face my fears and leave the relative safety of my living pod to speak with the snake people. If not for myself, then for my clients.

I had built a career navigating the capriciousness of entitled men. It seemed males weren't that different, no matter the species. It was disheartening, but I wasn't one to quit. If the Space Orcs thought they could manage me or tell me what to do, they had another think coming.

*"Yo no soy ninguna nena. ¡Soy una mujer, carajo!"* I would not be controlled by anyone or anything.

***

Seeing no other options, I cautiously left the pod and walked tentatively through the hallway, looking for the central gathering area. I knew I was housed somewhere in the guest quarters of the Royal Palatial Compound. When I was first told this, I thought it was a good sign that my clients must have powerful friends in the Nyokan court, but now I wondered if that was true or not.

As I walked down the thoroughfare, two young snake-children ran past me. Seeing my agitation, they both stopped, turned, and said in unison, "Sorry, my bad."

Okay, so I knew the universal translation chip was good, but why would the translation come out using human slang like "my bad" instead of something more formal like "I apologize"?

I continued walking, not sure exactly where I was going, when two more children, laughing, ran toward me from the opposite direction and stopped. What was curious, though, was that these children weren't Nyokan. They were mixed-race human boys, a beautiful combination of Black and Asian features. They appeared to be preteens, or maybe a little younger or older. I was never really sure with kids. They looked very similar, so they were probably twins. In any event, I was happy to see non-snake people, no matter what their age was.

"Hi, I'm Jabari," one said, grinning.

"I'm Jelani," said the other.

"Hi, I'm J.J.," I replied.

"Just like us," they said together, beaming.

"I didn't know other humans lived here," I said, still surprised.

"Yeah, we're not human though. Not completely," Jabari said.

"Not completely. Only Mom is all human," Jelani added.

"You're Nyokan?" I asked, hardly believing it.

"Fifty-fifty," Jabari said.

"They call us hybrids," Jelani said, clearly proud.

"We can switch forms," they said together, looking delighted.

"You wanna see?" Jabari asked.

"Um, no," I said, holding up a hand. "The form you have right now is great."

"Yeah," Jelani said. "You already saw us anyway, when we ran past you."

"That was you?" I asked.

"Yep," they both said.

"Are you lost?" Jelani asked, studying me.

"How could you tell?" I asked with a smile.

"We're smart," Jabari said, puffing his chest slightly.

"Well, that I could tell right away," I said.

"We can help you," Jelani offered. "Where do you want to go?"

"I'm looking for two Pstoady scientists named Torvak and Tovak. Do you know who they are?"

"Yep, we do," Jabari said. "T and T."

"Do you think you can take me to them? Unless of course it's too late," I asked.

"No, it's not too late," Jelani said.

"We just gotta hide from the sisters," Jabari added, lowering his voice.

"Yeah," Jelani said. "The sisters are mean."

"Do you mean your sisters?" I asked.

"Yeah," they both said together. "Big sisters are the worst."

I couldn't help laughing at these perfectly ordinary little boys in this alien setting.

"Okay, well help me find the Pstoadys," I said. "And if we see your sisters, I'll tell them what nice young men you were to help me."

"She called us young men," Jelani whispered.

"The sisters call us 'little coils,'" Jabari said, rolling his eyes.

"Well, I just see two very mannerable young men helping me find my friends," I said. "Let's go right away."

"Okay," said Jelani. "Do you want to run?"

"Yeah, let's run," Jabari said, already bouncing.

"How about we walk?" I suggested. "Humans aren't that fast. I might not be able to keep up."

"Yeah," Jelani said. "Just like Momma."

"Exactly," I said, smiling.

I followed the twin boys through the maze of the palace, staying mostly out of sight.

I had clearly found the best two conspirators around to help me circumvent the Space Orcs' directives.

We walked for about twenty minutes, and I was starting to get tired when Jelani—or was it Jabari—announced, "We're here."

I wasn't sure if we were in the main compound or not, but the boys were excited nonetheless.

They placed their hands on the door and a chime sounded.

"It's us!" Jabari said.

"Let us in!" Jelani added.

The door opened to reveal a futuristic-looking science lab.

Two small figures, about the same height as Jelani and Jabari, came into view.

They wore long white lab coats that covered them from just under their toad-like jowls to the tips of their clawed toes. They had huge, bulbous eyes on either side of their brownish-gray, toadlike heads. I'd read that they were often described as looking cartoon-like, and I had to agree.

Amazingly, they didn't seem surprised to see me, especially considering the unconventional way I'd arrived.

"Judge Judith Jimenez Jackson, welcome to our lab," the taller of the aliens said.

"I am Torvak," he added.

"And I am Tovak," said the other.

"It's just J.J.," I replied, trying to sound casual.

"You seem flustered, J.J.," Tovak said.

"Yes," I admitted with a breath.

"May we offer you refreshment?" they said together.

I suddenly realized I was starving. I'd slept for hours, argued with Space Orcs, and trekked through the compound with my twin hybrid conspirators.

"I'm not really thirsty," I said. "But do you have any standard galactic fare?"

"Yes, we have programmed our meal selections," said Tovak.

Torvak input a few codes, and a large Mediterranean salad appeared, complete with dressing.

"This is a favorite of Ambassador Vivien Johnson, also of Earth," said Tovak.

"You know Ambassador Johnson?" I asked surprised but somehow comforted that they were familiar with human beings, especially someone I knew.

"We shared a passage to the General Assembly in Quadrant Four a few annums past," said Torvak.

"We know her well," they said together.

I noticed that my clients sometimes spoke in unison and sometimes volleyed back and forth, almost like a tennis match. I smiled at the thought and focused more on listening to their unusual cadence.

"I know Vivien. Well, we know of each other," I replied. "Our paths often crossed when I was on the bench at the World Court."

"Ambassador Johnson now resides on Orcqlaneasus," said Tovak.

"You will like it there," added Torvak.

I took the salad and immediately dug in. I hadn't realized how hungry I was until then.

"I thought the goal was not to go to Orcqlaneasus," I said. "Did something change?"

"No," said Torvak.

"We cannot travel there yet," said Tovak.

"Our experiment has not concluded," they said together.

"Experiment?" I asked, looking up. "Are you running one here on Nyokaa?"

"No, not here," said Tovak.

"We conduct research here," said Torvak.

"We analyze our results here and recalibrate for best outcomes," they said together.

I listened casually as I ate. I was completely famished, and in seconds, I had polished off the huge salad.

"I think I'd like something to drink now, if you have it," I said.

"Yes, of course," said Torvak.

Tovak handed me a tall, cool, fruity drink. It tasted like something between a hurricane cocktail and mango juice. Whatever it was, it was delicious, and I slurped it down in seconds.

I looked around and realized the twin boys were nowhere in sight.

"Where are the boys?" I asked.

"Do you mean Prince Jelani and Prince Jabari?" said Tovak.

"They are sons of the royal family," said Torvak.

"Their aunt is the Scion, and their older brothers are next in line to rule Nyokaa," they said together.

"I had no idea," I murmured.

"They left shortly after they brought you," said Torvak.

"You were already engaged in conversation," added Tovak.

"Well, I don't know how I'll find my way back," I said. "But while I'm here, let's talk about your case."

"All will be fine," said Tovak.

"We can discuss the case tomorrow," said Torvak.

"It is quite late," they said together.

I rose from the table and immediately felt my stomach cramp.

"Are you alright, Judge J.J.?" asked Tovak.

"I think I ate too fast," I said. "But you're right, we'll talk tomorrow."

"I really have no idea how to get back without the boys," I added.

"We've ordered a conveyance for you," said Torvak.

"It will return you to your living pod," said Tovak.

"We programmed it ourselves," they said together.

I walked out and saw a sleek, wheel-less cart waiting for me. It was small, silver, and humming faintly. The Pstoadys keyed in the coordinates. We agreed to meet again the following afternoon, and they promised to send the same transport discreetly.

I sat in the smooth padded seat and almost instantly fell asleep.

I awoke to a soft chime at my pod door indicating I had arrived.

Inside my living pod, I finally took stock of the space. There was a lavatory, shower, bathing unit, and sleeping pod. Thankfully, my luggage had already been delivered.

I meant to shower before bed, as always, but I was too tired and too achy. I collapsed into the sleeping pod and closed my eyes.

That night, I had the most vivid and erotic dreams of my life.

*It began with heat, surrounding me, and a presence both mysterious and familiar. It was someone I had met only hours before, the Space Orc, Elder Nerisch.*

*He was over me, around me, everywhere. I didn't see him. I didn't need to. His body weighed heavy on mine, commanding, and possessive. His sharp claws gripped my hips as he dragged me open, like he knew I wanted him, knew I was already wet.*

*When his mouth descended, I nearly screamed.*

*His tongue was hot and thick, dragging against my clit, then plunging deeper, sucking like he was trying to devour me whole. My fingers found his braids, thick and coarse and impossibly long, and I gripped them hard, needing something to hold onto. My thighs trembled and my breath caught. I convulsed against his mouth as the first climax hit, hard and fast.*

*"¡Coño!"*

*One climax followed another. My body kept unraveling, no pause, no mercy, just the relentless pull of his mouth and the punishing grip of his claws. I sobbed as I came again, the sound raw, and the pleasure past bearing.*

*Then he moved.*

*He lifted me effortlessly, turned me, bent me forward onto my knees. My chest sank into some kind of bedding, though it felt like nothing earthly. His clawed hand pressed between my shoulder blades. I felt the tip of him behind me, and then he drove in, hard, thick, and impossibly deep. He was too big, too much. The stretch made my eyes roll back.*

*I lifted my head to scream, but Elder Coervich caught my face in his clawed hand. Without hesitation, he guided my mouth to his leaking dick and pressed it inside. I moaned around him, overwhelmed, as Elder Nerisch slammed into me from behind and Elder Coervich buried himself in my throat.*

*Elder Nerisch's breath hit my back in short, hot bursts as he fucked me deeper, holding me in place, claws biting into my hips to keep me open, and still. I couldn't stop shaking. I couldn't stop clenching around him. I couldn't stop the waves crashing through me, each orgasm slamming into the next.*

*He came with a deep, guttural growl, grinding hard against me, spilling deep inside me.*

*Elder Nerisch pulled out, thick and slow, his cum dripping down my thighs. I barely had time to breathe before another presence took his place, heavier, colder, just as commanding.*

*It was Elder Helvich.*

*I felt the press of him at my entrance, a harder shape, unfamiliar and demanding, stretching me wider than I thought I could go. Then he thrust in, deep and hard. I screamed around Elder Coervich's dick and he laughed. The burn inside was immediate. I tensed under it, overwhelmed by the way Elder Helvich filled me. He moved with no patience, no buildup, just force.*

*Each thrust sent shockwaves through me, slamming my ass back into him and my mouth forward onto Elder Coervich. I gagged with my throat stretched tight, spit sliding from my lips. My moans sounded raw and unfamiliar, like they came from a version of me that I had never encountered before. My body shook from the sheer force of it all.*

*Elder Helvich gripped me harder. His claws bit into my skin as he pounded into me. Each stroke triggered another orgasm, and I couldn't stop cumming. I screamed around Elder Coervich again. My body seized as everything broke inside me.*

*I felt Elder Coervich slow down and then erupt down my throat. I struggled not to choke as Elder Helvich fucked me through my climaxes, until he finally crashed into his own. He poured inside me, thick liquid heat. My body clenched again, overstretched and slick, barely able to contain it.*

And then the dream ended.

I woke up with my thighs soaked, out of breath, my heart racing. The memory of their bodies still burned into my skin. The ache between my legs was sharp and persistent. I was embarrassed, needy, and angry at the Space Orcs, and how they were so prescient in my mind that I had turned them into the ultimate dream lovers.

# CHAPTER 4: Elder Coervich Thaloryn - Space Orc

"Where is Nerisch?" I asked my bound brother, Helvich. Nerisch was never where he was supposed to be, and no matter the mission, agenda, or even the time of day, he was always either missing in action or creating his own action.

"He left earlier to meet with the Asani family, before our appointment this morning with the human," Helvich said.

"I did not realize we were scheduled to see her again. I thought we were arranging to take charge of the Pstoadys and ensure the female returned to Earth before she embroiled herself any further in Orcqlaneasion affairs," I said, confused by this change in events.

I generally handled all logistical matters, and securing both the Pstoady and Earth aliens fell within my purview.

"I struggled to sleep last night, so I set a more direct course of action," Helvich admitted.

Seeing my displeasure, he continued, "I found our encounter with the human female unsettling. I thought it best to act with haste, although I will defer to your judgment if my plans seem incomplete."

I understood the quandary my brother found himself in. I too had struggled to settle my thoughts regarding the human female. She did not defer. She questioned. She resisted. She behaved as though her will carried weight here.

Her beauty was irrelevant. What concerned me was her refusal to acknowledge risk, her insistence on pursuing a path she did not fully understand. It was not courage. It was recklessness. And I had no patience for it.

"I understand the need for haste in this matter, brother. The sooner the human is no longer our concern and sent on her way back to her homeworld, the better. I too found her presence to be, as you have said, unsettling," I conceded. "Does Nerisch's absence factor into your plan?"

"Yes, I asked Nerisch to handle the matter of having the Pstoadys released into our custody through his contacts with the ruling family, to avoid making a formal request through diplomatic channels," he said.

"Your plan is sound, brother," I said, easing the tension between us. "Have you made plans for the human as well?" I asked, curious to see if his thoughts aligned with mine.

"I sent a message via comms last night informing her that we would arrive later this morning to finalize the details of her departure from Nyokaa and return to Earth," he said.

I agreed that it was the most direct course of action, although based on our previous encounter with the human, it would not be well received. Before I could voice my concerns, an alert sounded on the comms, notifying us of Nerisch's imminent arrival.

"It looks like Nerisch has returned, but I do not read any additional life signatures. If he failed in his task, he will no doubt be intractable," Helvich said with a sigh.

Nerisch was more often than not ruled by emotion first and logic second. A win was celebrated with laughter and merriment. A loss was grieved with anger and hostility. His return without the Pstoady scientists likely meant he had been unsuccessful in his efforts to take the aliens into custody.

Anticipating the worst, we braced for Nerisch's arrival. Surprisingly, he sauntered in, looking completely relaxed and unconcerned.

I waited for him to speak, but when several minutes passed with no report, I confronted him, exasperated. "Brother, do not keep us in suspense. Tell us of your meeting with the Dukari twins."

"All is well, brothers. Dukari will assist us in quietly removing the Pstoadys from Nyokaa. They have them under surveillance and isolated under house arrest. We need only take custody of them and we are free to leave," he said smugly.

"That seems almost too easy. How were you able to convince them to circumvent their stringent asylum laws and place the aliens into our custody?" I asked.

"That part was a little tricky. I explained to them that discretion and haste were needed in handling this matter due to the nature of the Pstoadys' experimentation. I told them that the victims of all the Pstoadys' experiments were females much like their Kayla. Once they learned this, they wanted the scientists removed from Nyokaa with all due speed," he said confidently.

"That is excellent news, brother. It seems Helvich's plan to send you to negotiate the Pstoadys' release into our custody was sound indeed. Now we have only the matter of sending the human on her way back to Earth, and we will have accomplished our mission and can return to Orcqlaneasus," I said, proud of my brother's accomplishment.

The comms signaled an incoming call, and our brief celebration was cut short.

Answering the call, we were greeted with the twin visages of Dukari$^{1}$ and Dukari$^{2}$, along with the unexpected appearance of their youngest offspring, Jabari and Jelani Asani.

Seeing the young ones, Nerisch immediately responded with a greeting. The young Nyokans drooped their scaly heads and did not return it. Immediately, I sensed something was amiss.

"Our sons have news that you need to hear. It may affect your mission," Dukari$^{2}$ said.

We waited to see what the little coils would reveal, but both seemed hesitant.

"Sons, tell them what mischief you've caused," Dukari$^{1}$ prompted.

The small Nyokans stood beside each other, one with scales of shimmering copper-gold, the other with sparkling emerald green. Unlike their sires, their faces appeared more humanoid, thanks to their mother from Earth. In typical youthful fashion, each nudged the other to speak, but neither took the lead. When nudging didn't work, they began hissing at each other in frustration. Before they devolved into a full-blown snake fight, their fathers intervened.

"Jabari, speak," Dukari$^{2}$ said, elongating the sibilant sound in a clear sign of his irritation.

"Last night, we were hiding from the sisters," Jabari began.

"They said we stank and needed to bathe," Jelani added, jumping in to support his brother despite their earlier disagreement.

"We ran through the courtyard and saw the female, the one like Mama," Jabari continued.

"She seemed scared when she saw us, so we came back. But this time, we looked like we were from her planet," Jelani added.

"She asked us for help finding her friends," Jabari said quietly, pausing to gauge our reaction.

Immediately, I knew the direction their tale was headed and was reluctant to hear more.

Nerisch gently coaxed the twins to continue. His praise emboldened them, and they straightened with pride.

Their sires, recognizing Nerisch's subtle manipulation to keep the younglings talking, exchanged a grimace and a slow tongue flick.

Encouraged, Jelani picked up where his brother left off. "We told her we knew the Pstoadys she was looking for and took her there, through the shadows."

"Through the shadows?" Dukari[1] asked, concern in his tone.

"The shadows are the spots where the royal cams can't see us, so Iyana and Iyala can't find us and tell Mama," Jabari admitted, hanging his head.

Nerisch interjected to keep the mood light. "Brilliant, you avoided the cams. Did you arrive at the Pstoadys' residence?"

"No, we took her to their lab," Jelani said. "They gave her food, and we left."

"It was getting late, so we went back home before Mama found out and got upset," Jabari added, glancing nervously at his sires.

Despite myself, I asked, "Did she return to her assigned quarters?"

Dukari[1] entered a command into the console, and a live feed appeared, showing the human asleep in a unicraft en route to her guest unit. We watched silently as the craft arrived and she entered the residence.

I exhaled a breath I hadn't realized I was holding.

Dukari[2] dismissed his sons, promising a conversation about their behavior later.

"In light of what you shared with us earlier, I cannot think this new development bodes well for your human female," Dukari[1] said.

Helvich confirmed, "Based on their past encounters with human females, they have almost certainly dosed her with the breeding pheromone. We will need to collect her, along with the Pstoadys, and return to Orcqlaneasus immediately."

The Dukari brothers exchanged a look before addressing us again.

"Apologies for the indelicacy, but are you planning on breeding her?" Dukari[1] asked.

"No," I replied at once. While this specific outcome had not been anticipated, contingencies were in place. "We have a stasis unit already programmed for human female biological life support. Once we return to Orcqlaneasus, more options will be available based on the research of Dr. Nina Bridges."

"Is there any assistance we can offer? Given our sons' involvement, we feel obligated to help," Dukari[1] said.

"Unfortunately, there is nothing you can do. We will contact Orcqlaneasus to update them and alert them of this new development," Helvich replied.

"Perhaps it would be easier for her to hear this news from one of her own kind. We can dispatch our mate to assess her condition and explain the infection," Dukari[2] offered.

The relief among us was palpable.

"The assistance of Lady Kayla in this instance would be greatly appreciated. I will send her the comms information to contact Dr. Bridges on Orcqlaneasus," Helvich said.

"There is no need. Kayla has already been in contact with the human females on your planet, including Ambassador Vivien Johnson and Dr. Nina Bridges," Dukari$^2$ said.

That revelation surprised us, though perhaps it should not have.

"We will dispatch our mate and contact you with a resolution," Dukari$^2$ concluded before ending the transmission.

# CHAPTER 5: J.J. No Pain No Gain

I've been in pain before. In fact, I have a pretty high tolerance for it. And by that, I in no way mean to pay homage to the stereotype that Black people, Black women in particular, can tolerate extreme pain, because that is completely untrue.

As pain went, though, I had muscle memory that ran pretty deep, based in no small part on the loss of my babies. I'd miscarried a total of five times while I was married to William. Each had been painful in its own way. There was joy and expectation at first, but loss and grief eventually followed. One stood out from the others as hell on Earth. Imagine carrying a baby to term, having a baby shower, opening gifts, setting up a nursery, seeing her moving on the ultrasound, and giving my beautiful little girl a name, Carina. Then imagine coming home from the hospital in agony, alone. The weight of it was so oppressive. I was smothered in sorrow and misery and couldn't rouse myself to get out of bed for weeks.

My heart was broken, and after that so was my marriage. I eventually pushed through the pain and found solace in my career, working on average more than 90 hours per week. I pushed the pain away, pushed my family away, and pushed my husband away. Yes, I knew pain. *El dolor y yo... éramos uña y carne.*

And now, decades later, I felt the dull blade of pain again, in a familiar yet strange new way. I woke up from a restless slumber, disheveled, drenched in perspiration. My mind seared with erotic images that I tried to block out.

Tossing and turning in the alien sleeping pod made no sense at all, so I gritted my teeth through the sharp, contraction-like cramps assaulting my barren womb and made my way to the lav unit. I felt much more human after showering and getting dressed, although the shooting pain was still present.

I was searching frantically for pain relievers in my luggage when I heard the incessant chirp of the entrance chime alerting me that I had an unexpected guest. In my current state, I was in no condition to spar with the Space Orcs, so I sent up a small prayer that it wasn't them.

I went to the door panel and waved my hand across it as I had done the previous night and, just like before, it opened. This time, however, it wasn't the dreaded Space Orcs but another human. She was a pretty middle-aged Black woman with a sprinkling of grey hair throughout her curly afro. I opened my mouth to greet her, but a cramp tore through my body, causing me to fold over.

"It's okay, everything will be alright," the stranger said, rushing in, lending me her sizable strength, preventing me from falling over.

She ushered me over to a sitting pod, where I curled into a ball on myself, clutching my abdomen.

"What can I do? How can I help you? I have a hypospray if you think that might help," the helpful stranger said.

I didn't know who she was or anything about her other than she offered me help, and in my current state, all I could do was mumble my acceptance of her offer.

She handed me the hypospray, and I placed it on my stomach and depressed the plunger. Immediately, I felt a surge of relief as the pain left my body. I took a couple of deep breaths and composed myself long enough to address the kind stranger.

"Thank you for helping me," I said, managing to compose myself. With the pain fast retreating, I felt overcome by embarrassment.

"It's no problem at all, and to be quite honest, I feel responsible for how you're feeling right now, if even indirectly," she said. Before I could puzzle out her statement, she continued in haste.

"I know what that must sound like, so let me explain. I'm Kayla Asani. I believe you met my youngest two sons last night in the courtyard."

Suddenly, it all made much more sense. She was the parent of the precocious pre-teens who had helped me find my clients yesterday.

"You're Jabari and Jelani's mom. They were a godsend to me last night. I was absolutely lost in this maze of a palace," I said with all sincerity.

I noticed that instead of looking pleased, my benefactor looked stricken. It was the kind of look that was usually followed by bad news.

"I'm really sorry that my sons got you involved, but they had no idea. Actually, they still have no idea. They just know they're in hot water for roaming through the palace when they were supposed to be under the supervision of their older sisters."

"They did mention something about sisters last night, but did something happen? Are they okay?" I asked, instantly worried about my little hybrid guides.

Looking around, Kayla said, “Um, I need to sit, you don’t mind, do you?”

She pulled a seating pod directly in front of me and held my hand. Immediately, I felt a sense of déjà vu. I was reminded again of all that I’d lost before. I took a deep breath.

“I know something’s wrong. Go ahead and tell me,” I said, squeezing her hand.

She nodded and began. “A little over a year ago, the Pstoadys came to our planet seeking refuge. They were being chased by Orcqlaneasion assassins, and my older two sons, Kamari and Kajari, intervened and granted them asylum. At the time, the Space Orcs didn’t give us a full accounting of what the Pstoadys had done, keeping it all very hush-hush, and we allowed the scientists to stay here, presumably so that we could keep an eye on them.” She paused and pinched the bridge of her nose before continuing.

"If I had known what they were planning, I never would have allowed it. Honestly, they might have tried it on me too. But with all the venom in my system, I doubt it would have worked. I don’t know. The Orcqlaneasions kept us in the dark."

She rubbed her palms together and glanced away.

"The scientists seemed harmless, like model residents. That’s how my little coils got close to them. They were always polite, always helpful. They even tutored my boys in basic galactic science."

She paused again, then met my eyes.

"I’m sorry. It’s hard to say this out loud. They thought it would be easier coming from me," she said quietly.

"Who thought?" I asked, though I already knew the answer. It had to be those overbearing elder aliens I met yesterday.

“The Orcqlaneasions, Space Orcs. Up until recently, their species was facing extinction. There were only about a thousand of them left, scattered throughout the four known quadrants of space as peacekeepers. During the Distant Wars, Space Orcs served as security on medical space stations that treated soldiers and civilians. The Pstoadys were stationed at one of those facilities too. While working under their human director, they discovered a solution to the Orcqlaneasions' reproductive problem. They created a pheromone that, when administered to a human female, specifically a Black human female, makes her capable of procreating with Orcqlaneasions and giving birth to their children."

I listened intently as she narrated the circumstances of the Pstoadys assisting the Orcqlaneasions with their reproduction issues, but still couldn't understand her obvious distress in recounting the events. If anything, it proved that my clients had no ill intention toward the Orcqlaneasions.

"I understand, but from what you've said, I can't see why the Space Orcs would be hunting down the Pstoadys, with assassins, no less," I said. I tried to think back on all the research I'd done on both species to help me in my upcoming negotiations. Nothing came to mind, although I felt like I'd seen something that alluded to reproduction somewhere, but the cramps accelerated in strength and intensity as though an invisible knife was jaggedly carving itself in my uterus.

Unintentionally, I gave Kayla's hand a hard squeeze. It felt like I was having contractions. She covered my hand with her other hand and looked at me sadly.

"They told me the hyposprays wouldn't last long, but I was hoping you'd have relief long enough to understand what's happening and consider stasis. It's the only way to keep your symptoms from escalating."

"Stasis? What symptoms? What the hell are you talking about?" I asked as the waves of pain abated slightly.

"I'm afraid you've been infected with the alien pheromone the Pstoadys created, and the cramping you're feeling is a symptom of your body going into estrus or heat. Apparently, it's like ovulation in the extreme. It compels you to want sex, and it also allows your body to stretch to accommodate them; the Orcqlaneasions," she said with a pained, hesitant expression.

I was dumbfounded. She couldn't mean that I was infected. My clients had seen ME as a potential breeder. What had they done to me? I'd been lured to a strange planet as some sort of human incubator. Suddenly, with a flash of clarity, I remembered the NDA that my client, Sunni Davis, had signed specifically regarding "interspecies initiative participation." Had this been her fate? Had I unwittingly been part of some intergalactic human trafficking ring? Was the kind woman in front of me my handler, brought to ease me into my new life as a breeder?

I couldn't believe what was happening, but it was crystal clear, and she was part of it. Her half-breed offspring had delivered me to the Pstoadys. They were all working together. I snatched my hand from her grasp. I wanted no part of these aliens and this human bitch that was obviously collaborating with them.

I screamed at her while taking big, gulping breaths as I struggled to breathe between the incessant cramping. "Why did you do this to me, all of you? I'm human, and I won't be turned into some alien broodmare making little half-breed monsters."

All my pain and fear came rushing to the surface as my words lashed out at the human woman who had only moments before pretended to be my benefactor. For all I knew, she'd injected me with more of the pheromone the aliens had created.

My body shook as my mind grappled with what was happening to my body. Despite my vicious words, she reached out to me as if to embrace me, but I rejected it. I rejected her and everything that was happening to me.

"Don't touch me. What have you done to me? ¡Eres una bruja maldita!" I screamed.

In the next heartbeat, I was facing down a nightmare come to life. Two six-and-a-half-foot viper snakes surrounded me, poised to attack. I screamed from the depths of my soul, paralyzed in fear. In slow motion, I saw the witch sent to comfort me wildly waving her arms as she placed her body between me and the vicious snake creatures. Overcome with fright, my body seized in the clutches of pain, and I fell deep into darkness, away from everything.

# CHAPTER 6: Elder Nerisch Braedaris - Space Orc

Taking custody of the two small Pstoady scientists that had wrought so much havoc to our society was an event that was anticlimactic. The two figures posed no visible threat that I could see, and I struggled to understand how they had eluded captivity both by Orcqlaneasions of Warrior class and Elder class alike.

The Pstoadys were conveyed to our ship by two Nyokan Royal Guardians, the elite force of the Nyokan military. Peacefully and without resistance, I placed them in the newly retrofitted confinement bay that had been upgraded especially for this mission: containment of the Pstoady scientists. Surrounded by my brethren, and with no words spoken, the diminutive aliens shuffled into the restrictive compartment that would hold them until we returned to Orcqlaneasus.

Making sure the locking mechanisms were in place and vid cams operational to ensure there would be no way to possibly escape, my brethren and I returned to the bridge.

"Coervich, send a long-range communication to the Directorate letting them know that we have secured the Pstoadys," Helvich ordered from his command post.

Immediately, Coervich complied, sending the message along with our estimated time of arrival.

"Nerisch, contact Dukari and their mate, for an update on our recalcitrant human," he sighed. I knew that neither Helvich nor Coervich had any interest in mating the human female, so I attempted to conform my thoughts to theirs.

It was not the first time in the many years that I had been with my brothers that I was required had to modify my actions to remain attuned to theirs. It was something that I accepted long ago, not quite understanding how we had been bonded as a unit in the first place, nevertheless accepting my fate.

In our time as warriors, when we all lived by the warrior's code, it was easier to be in one accord with my brethren. But now, as we had matured into Elder class, it was difficult for me, although not for them, to act more judiciously and settle into a life of quiet contemplation. I did not want to be a diplomat or an ambassador for my people in Quadrant Four. While here on Quadrant Three, the atmosphere was less formal. Yes, there were different alien species to contend with, but the ruling order of Nyokaa, our ally, primarily held sway over all factions.

Befriending the Dukari twins as they took on the role of diplomats, following the path set by their parents, made the assignment on Quadrant Three no hardship at all. I mentored their irrepressible elder sons, and watched in awe as they were manipulated endlessly by their daughters. Finding out the latest antics their little coils had been involved in was not surprising at all, having witnessed their other offspring over the years. Quadrant Three had been the sector we were assigned as Warriors and continued on as Elders. Being called to leave it and go to a diplomatic post on Quadrant Four was an elevation that my bound brothers were more than pleased with. I would, however, miss my time with my friends and their children.

As I mused on my circumstance, an urgent call came through the comms from the Dukari twins.

"Dukari, how did the meeting with Lady Kayla and the human legal representative go?" I asked.

Dukari[1], the calmer of the twins, answered my query with measured words, his anger apparent in the way that he held his body, lethal, as if ready to strike.

"Not well. The human verbally attacked our mate. She has been expelled from our planet. A shuttle will be arriving shortly to deliver her to your ship," he said perfunctorily.

Coervich responded immediately. "Our ship, are you delivering her to us?" he questioned.

"Yes, the human is no longer welcome on our planet. Make sure she is out of our space within the hour," Dukari[2] said, hostilely.

Seeing the seriousness of the situation, I intervened with my old friends, hoping to avoid an intergalactic incident that would be hard to come back from.

"We will receive the human and expedite her removal from Nyokaa. How fares Lady Kayla?" I asked, attempting for once to be diplomatic and alleviate the simmering hostility.

Lady Kayla appeared on-screen, with a welcoming smile, her usual countenance.

"I'm fine, but I'm afraid Dukari overreacted and almost attacked the woman. She didn't take the news of being infected well at all. She thinks it's some kind of intergalactic breeding conspiracy and we're all a part of it," she explained, wringing her hands.

"She insulted my love. Our children. Had our mate not intervened..." Dukari[1] stopped short, his wrath coming to the forefront.

"Dukari, it's okay. She was scared, more than that actually. She passed out in sheer terror. Apparently, in addition to everything else, she has a phobia when it comes to snakes. It's best that she leave Nyokaa for her own safety," Lady Kayla explained.

A klaxon rang, alerting us of the shuttle's arrival. Hearing it, the Nyokans and their mate visibly relaxed.

"I never got the chance to tell her about being put into stasis," Lady Kayla said.

"She is not in stasis? Is she infected?" Helvich asked.

"Yes, she's definitely infected, but she was in no state to decide anything, and I didn't think it was right to place her in cold stasis without her consent. Perhaps the scientists can offer a remedy once they see the result of their actions on an unwilling participant," she reasoned.

Before my brothers could dissent and cause more of a problem, I concurred with Lady Kayla's assessment. "I agree. She should be able to decide the next course of action. Having the Pstoadys on board should give us more options for treatment or an antidote to the pheromones affecting her."

Helvich interjected, "We will accept the human and return to Orcqlaneasus. Thank you for your discernment in this matter."

Lady Kayla wished us luck, and the Asani family signed off, leaving us to handle the new problem of the infected human female currently being placed on our ship.

"I will see to the human's arrival and secure her in a stateroom," Coervich said reluctantly.

"I will go with you, brother, in case the human proves too much for you to handle," I joked.

"I do not see the humor in your statement, brother. Rather than a stateroom, we should place her in stasis until we arrive in Orcqlaneasus," Helvich added.

"Yes, that is a better idea," Coervich agreed.

Again, I found myself at odds with my brethren. "I believe Lady Kayla's reasoning was sound. We should not take away the human's choice whether to be placed in stasis or not."

"There is no point in continually drugging the human with hyposprays and sedatives until we arrive in Orcqlaneasus. The only acceptable solution is to place her into a stasis pod," Helvich said.

"At least give her the chance to understand the full extent of what is happening," I countered.

"I believe she should be placed in stasis immediately," Coervich added. "But we can approach her again. If she remains intractable, we proceed with stasis confinement."

We left our places on the bridge to meet our human guest, unsure of what to expect. When we arrived at the shuttle bay, two members of the Royal Guardians ushered out a medical hoverbed with the human asleep on it. We took possession of the female, and the Nyokans departed.

Without fanfare, we carried the human to a stateroom, where Helvich carefully laid her on the large bed. Since she remained asleep, the decision of whether to place her in stasis would have to wait. Through our bond I could feel our shared unrest about the mission, the Pstoady prisoners, the infected human, and my own dissent from my brethren. We left her alone. My brothers returned to their stations to prepare for the voyage home, and I made my way to the exercise bay, hoping to find the peace and harmony that should have come naturally in our bound brotherhood but rarely did.

# CHAPTER 7: J.J. The Sweetest Pain

I woke up disoriented and in complete darkness.

As my eyes slowly focused on the ambient light from the room, my body felt like it was on fire and I struggled to piece together where I was and what had happened to me. The last thing I remembered was the gigantic snake creatures towering over me before I passed out.

Somehow, I'd been moved from the Nyoka dwelling. I wasn't in a sleeping pod anymore, but a large bed. As I sat up, my body was once again pummeled with cramps, this time layered with something else. If what the witch, Kayla, had said was true, I was in the throes of heat. I ripped the clothing from my body, desperate for relief from the suffocating, inescapable heat. I thrashed on the bed, furious, panting, as waves of unfulfilled lust and ravenous hunger crashed through me. Objectively, I knew it was the pheromone they'd dosed me with to make me a breeder. Subjectively, I didn't give a damn. I just wanted to fuck.

In the darkened room, I wasn't alone. I felt eyes on me, heat rolling from a presence just out of reach. I zeroed in on it.

"Is this what you wanted? Why are you just standing there?" I shouted, breathless and angry. I was hot, raw, needy, twisted up in everything I hated and everything I craved.

I bent my knees and spread my legs. I didn't care if he watched. I stroked my pussy, thumbs gliding over my swollen lips before I slipped two fingers inside. I plucked at myself like strings on a guitar, each motion sending shocks of pleasure up my spine. I was drenched. My body convulsed as I pumped in and out, the slick sounds of my release obscene in the silence.

He emerged from the shadows.

I wanted to hate him. I wanted to hate this. But my body betrayed me, arching toward him before he even touched me. I needed him more than I'd ever needed anything in my life. Logically, I knew it was the drug. Emotionally, I didn't care. I was far past caring.

He was majestic. Easily over seven feet tall, his body radiated heat and dominance. His skin, in the dim light, looked like dark olive stone. He was powerful and commanding. The smirk on his face matched the expression I remembered, along with the long white braids that brushed his waist.

It was Nerisch Braedaris, one of the Orcqlaneasion Elders who had come to my quarters uninvited and full of authority, trying to forbid me from meeting the Pstoadys. I remembered his voice, the way he had loomed in my doorway, trying to intimidate me. I had ignored him then. But my subconscious hadn't. I had conjured him in my dreams, and now I knew that whatever was happening, I still couldn't ignore him.

He said nothing, not a single word. He gripped my wrist, pulled my slick fingers from between my legs, and sucked them into his mouth, licking each digit like he was tasting honey.

Then he bent and buried his face in my pussy. It was nothing like my dream.

I gasped. My back arched and my thighs spread wider as he feasted. His tongue licked everywhere, flicking my clit, teasing the sensitive skin, then plunging inside. He growled into me, the vibration rumbling through my pussy like thunder. He sucked, then flattened his tongue and dragged it slow, building pressure. Then he sucked my clit again, harder this time, and I shattered.

I came loud, body trembling. He didn't stop. His tongue circled my entrance, diving in again, over and over. He pulled more pleasure from me, more than I thought I had. His fangs grazed my skin, sharp but careful, and I cried out again, hands fisting the sheets.

He finally rose, his chin and mouth glistening with my release. I should have been satisfied. Instead, I burned hotter. I ached deeper.

He kissed my belly, my thighs, my stretch marks. They were reminders of what I'd once carried, and the memory jolted something in me. He wanted to breed me, to turn me into a vessel. Still, my body wanted him. Wanted his weight, his size, his seed. I hated myself for it.

He was fascinated with the marks on my belly. Maybe he saw them as scars from a failed battle. In truth, they were. I had lost the war to be a mother.

I pushed his face, hoping to turn it away.

Instead, I saw questions in his dark eyes.

"You carry scars. Here," he said, stroking the lingering line of an emergency caesarean from years ago.

I didn't want to think about it. But there was no way to avoid it. Maybe that was for the best.

"I was pregnant before," I said quietly. "More than once. None of my babies survived."

The words doused my passions briefly. I braced for rejection, already knowing the look I would see. I had lived it before in William's eyes, after each loss, until there was nothing left.

I shouldn't care what this alien thought. He was using me. That was their plan.

But still, I couldn't help wishing I could be what he wanted.

He gave no reply. Maybe that was best. He just kept touching me.

His fangs teased my nipples, scraping gently before he sucked them into his mouth. Pain and pleasure merged into a single spark. He moved up until his mouth found mine. I tasted myself in his kiss as he gripped my breasts in his clawed hands.

"You are called J.J. Is there a meaning for this?" he asked, voice low, rough, with a smoky edge that made my toes curl.

I could barely speak, breathless with want. "Judith Jackson. Or Judith Jiminez. The J sounds like an H sometimes. It used to be Judge Judith, but that title's long gone. So... just Judith."

His eyes locked with mine.

"Just Judith, will you take my seed, be my mate, share my lifeforce, and bear my sons?"

I wanted to say no. I wanted to tell him I couldn't do this, that I wasn't built for it. But I also wanted to believe. I wanted to be wanted this badly, even if none of it was real. And if it all fell apart, I could blame the drug, blame the aliens who had set this up.

I opened wider. My body answered before I could.

"Yes," I said, my voice low. "But I can't give you sons. You chose the wrong human to breed."

He pressed the thick head of his cock against me. The heat from it was unreal. He didn't push in. Not yet.

"Sons will come. And if they do not, you are still worthy. I will protect you, honor you, and cherish you. My bound brothers and I will share our lifeforce with you, but only with consent."

"I do."

He entered me slowly, stretching me inch by inch. My breath caught. He was too thick, too long. I hadn't had sex in years and this was beyond anything I'd ever taken. My body clenched, resisted, then softened around him. I gasped as he slid in deeper. The stretch bordered on pain, but I didn't want it to stop.

He held still, letting me adjust. His forehead pressed to mine. Then he began to move.

He fucked me hard, deep, and deliberate. His hips pounded into me with a rhythm that was perfect and relentless. My body rocked with every thrust, and I clung to his shoulders as he drove into me over and over. I couldn't think. I could barely breathe.

I came fast, screaming, clawing at him, but he didn't stop.

He flipped me over, raised my hips, and drove in from behind. I collapsed onto the bed, arms limp, while he held me by the waist and took what I'd already given. My moans turned to sobs as he filled me over and over.

He growled and buried himself deep, and I felt him come. His cum poured into me, hot and thick, flooding my barren womb. I squeezed around him, greedy for every drop.

He held still, arms locked around me as we both came down. I collapsed against his chest, dazed, barely breathing.

The cramps had faded. The fever cooled to a slow, steady burn.

I had mated an alien. My fate was tied to his now, whatever that meant in this galaxy.

# CHAPTER 8: Helvich, The Mate

The rift with my bound brother Nerisch was a source of concern for me, and for Coervich as well. While Coervich often took time to weigh options carefully, Nerisch charged forward on instinct. If I leaned one way, Nerisch predictably leaned the other. Yet in all other matters, he had always yielded for the good of the collective. Never before had there been hesitation, defiance, or any move to countermand the will of the brotherhood, until now.

This confirmed to me yet again the danger of associating with human females. Nerisch had always been different, even when we took our sacred vows more than sixty annums ago. But until now, his unpredictability had never posed a threat to our unity.

That was why, the moment I felt the lift in my spirits caused by Nerisch's euphoria, I did not suspect what should have been obvious. I was accustomed to Nerisch's battle games, which he re-enacted in great detail in the Exercise Bay, often spiking our adrenaline with bursts of positive energy. But this was more intense, more prolonged.

I turned to Coervich to ask whether he felt the same elation emanating from Nerisch. His nod in return confirmed that he did, without the need for words between us.

"Computer, where is Elder Nerisch Braedaris?" I asked, hoping for a response that he was still in the Exercise Bay.

"Elder Nerisch Braedaris is currently in Diplomatic Stateroom Sigma Seven," the A.I. voice replied.

Before the thought could fully form in my mind, Coervich spoke it aloud. "He could not have done this; not without consulting us."

I agreed, my anger at this turn of events magnified by my bound brother's shared emotional link. A solution that called for anything less than hand-to-hand combat was not readily apparent.

"I will go to the stateroom. I must confirm that what I dread has not actually occurred," I said.

"There can be no other explanation for what we are feeling. Nerisch has mated the human without our consent. This was never an option we discussed; ever," Coervich raged.

"I cannot imagine that Nerisch would recklessly jeopardize our sacred bond after so many years. Let us go together and retrieve our brother. As I suspected, the influence of these human females is dangerous to our brotherhood. Nothing proves it more than this," I reasoned.

Securing the ship with computer navigation and autopilot engaged, we went to wrest our brother from the clutches of the human female.

***

Stepping into the stateroom, we were assaulted with the overpowering scent of sex, sweat, and musk. Admittedly it was a powerful combination, but one I steeled myself against.

Impossible to resist, though, was the scene playing out before us. The human, J.J., was riding our brother's cock, her back arched and head thrown back, sweat glistening across her honey-golden skin. Her gray and black curls cascading down her back. Nerisch's claws gripped her ass, fingers flexing with each bounce. Her moans echoed off the walls, matched only by the deep growls rising from his chest.

I called out to my brother, but no words left my mouth, only a growl of my own, low and guttural. Need surged through me. I stripped off my white Elder's robes and approached the enchanting human.

She turned her head slightly, eyes clear, lips parted. Her gaze met mine. There was no hesitation, only want, a silent invitation.

I stood before her, cock heavy and leaking, each throb begging for her mouth. I reached down and traced her lower lip with the head of my spearhead cock.

She opened willingly.

Her tongue flicked out first, tasting me. She licked slowly, savoring the scent rising between us, clean and sharp with a hint of mint that marked our kind. She sealed her lips around the tip, a soft moan escaping as the first drop met her tongue.

Her lips stretched wide as she worked to take more of me. Inch by inch, she fed herself my cock, but its girth and size restricted her progress as my spearhead lodged itself in the confines of her tight throat. She struggled to breathe, her eyes watered, but she didn't stop. She gagged softly, then moaned again, both hands gripping my thighs as she tried to take me in deeper. Her spit poured over her chin, messy and uncontrolled, and still she fought to take more, lips bruising, jaw aching, her throat fluttering helplessly around me.

Below her, Nerisch growled and thrust up into her soaked pussy, forcing her to ride him faster. She was caught in a rhythm between us, my cock pressing into her throat while his stayed buried inside her warmth. She was whimpering now, breath ragged and desperate, her body shaking from too much stimulation. Her groans vibrated along my shaft, each one a fluttering tremor that made my balls tighten.

Feeling her moans caress my cock as she reached her climax, I couldn't hold back. I gripped her head, hips jerking forward as I emptied into her throat. My cum flooded her mouth, thick and hot as my brother likewise filled her pussy, releasing into her overwrought body. I slowly pulled out of her mouth. Her face was a mess of saliva, sweat, and my seed. She shuddered as Nerisch pulled out from her pussy. She lay on the bed alone, quivering, but still begging for more.

Coervich watched from just inside the doorway, his breath shallow, his eyes dark. He stepped into the room and silently began to undress.

Our previous sentiment about extracting Nerisch from her clutches was forgotten, we were further ensnared by the lure of our human mate, ours to be claimed.

J.J. reached out for him, fingers curling, wordless and wild with need.

Coervich came forward, now naked, his cock hard and leaking. He knelt at the head of the bed, pressing his tip to her mouth. She opened for him immediately, tongue out, lips soft. He pressed into her mouth without remorse or a moment's pause, ruthlessly fucking her throat as she gagged and groaned, no escape from his shuttling cock.

He thrust brutally forward as though trying to purge every conflicting impulse through her mouth. Her eyes rolled back, tears spilling down her cheeks. Quickly he released inside her, a growl tearing from his throat as he pulled away as though scorched by a laser's edge.

Dazed and confused, J.J. sat up helplessly watching as Coervich walked away. I felt his remorse, his shame, his satisfaction. He had pleasured himself with the human despite his belief that he would not. I knew the conflict that he felt, because I shared it. But still I was driven to bond with her, to mate her, to breed her and make her mine.

Pushing my sane thoughts away I gave into my instincts and lowered my body over hers, placing her legs over my shoulders and prepared to bury my seed and frustration deep inside her willing body.

Remembering our rites I spoke her name, "Judith Jiminez Jackson, by custom and deed I would claim you as my mate. Will you take my seed, bear my sons, and share my lifeforce?" I said the words I never expected to say in my time as Warrior, especially in my time as Elder and though the words came from my lips they were not emblazoned on my heart. I would mate the human because my brother had left me no choice, my body had left me no choice, but I vowed silently, I would give her my seed and nothing more.

She looked at me with warm brown eyes, as if she could see into my soul and knew my words were hollow, but still she responded. "I will."

Gaining her consent, I plowed into her with a force that shook her body, each thrust a war between duty and denial. My vow had been to share only my seed, but with each stroke the lie in that vow deepened.

I bared my fangs, reminding myself this was duty, not desire. But her body pulled me deeper, wet and yielding, clutching me like she already knew what I swore I would not give. I did not want to need her, but I did. Each thrust blurred the line between obligation and instinct, until the lie I had told myself crumbled beneath the truth of her.

Mercilessly, I fucked into this human vessel that was mine to fill with my seed. She had broken something within us, setting brother against another. For this she would receive a raw and ruthless reckoning as I poured my anger, distrust, and frustration into every thrust, ravaging her pussy not as an aging elder but as a brutal warrior of Orcqlaneasus.

I gripped her hips with bruising force, slamming into her over and over, her breath catching in ragged gasps, the wet slap of our bodies echoing off the walls. And even in my furious fucking I found pleasure in her as she found pleasure from me, her body convulsing over and over, clenching and releasing until I had no choice but to give in and flood her with my cum.

Ashamed, I immediately pulled from her, my body still shaken in the aftermath of the intensity. I wanted to leave, to place myself far away from her and my part in this mating ritual, but I could not. Coervich had not yet claimed her and my retreat would leave the mark of the event as incomplete. What Nerisch had started would need to be finished by Coervich.

As if sensing my thoughts, Coervich reluctantly approached our human mate. Seeing him move closer, she reached for him again, this time hesitantly, as though recalling the way he had walked away from her before.

He lifted her from the bed, and a gush of fluids slipped from her body. She looked embarrassed, but Coervich ignored it. He turned her over and laid her on her stomach, then pulled her up onto her hands and knees. He pushed her ass up, spreading her thighs wider with a grip that was impersonal, clinical. Positioning himself behind her, he spoke without emotion.

"J.J. from Earth, will you take my seed and be my mate?" he said flatly.

"Yes," she said in a low, steady voice.

He entered her without hesitation, surging forward with brutal force. It was retribution. A ritual carried out by someone trying to outrun his own instincts.

Did she deserve it? Unquestionably. Had she followed our directives, she would never have been infected. Her desires would not have turned into ours, and Nerisch would never have fucked her. Which meant none of us would have.

I wanted to turn away from the scene that had begun as sensual but had degenerated into punishment, for her and for us. We were committed to this course of action, if not to each other.

Coervich kept pumping, jaw clenched, breathing ragged. I could feel the conflict tearing through him. He had fought against this, told himself he would not. But now, inside her, he was unraveling.

His grip on her hips tightened. He pounded into her harder, as if trying to bury every shred of reluctance with each punishing stroke. Every movement was stripped of grace, reduced to raw drive and fury.

When he finally came, it was not pleasure that overtook him. It was release, a necessary evil to complete the act.

He pulled out immediately, as though she burned him from the inside. He did not look back. He grabbed his robes and rushed from the room.

Nerisch gathered her in his arms, and she went willingly, nestling into him. I picked up my garments and moved toward the door. I could hear her sobs as I reached the threshold. I turned back once. Nerisch held her to his chest as she cried quietly.

Although we had all mated her as demanded by custom, two of us had rejected her, leaving only Nerisch to console our human mate.

# CHAPTER 9: J.J. The Unseen War

That night, the first of many, I cried myself to sleep in the arms of my alien lover, my mate, Nerisch. I had never done that before. In the past, I always cried privately, hiding my pain from others. But since I had been infected, both Kayla the witch and my alien mate had seen me at my lowest point.

Honestly, I didn't care anymore. My logical, safe world had been turned upside down, and nothing made sense anymore. They were taking me back to their home planet, where I'd encounter other females who had been taken, bred, and trafficked for sex like I had been.

Even though they called it mating, I knew I wasn't on an equal footing with them. Nerisch was enamored with my body and comforted me for the pleasure it gave him.

The other two used me for release. I was nothing more than a receptacle for their alien sperm.

At least the awful cramps and high temperatures had lessened. I almost felt like myself again, with the exception being that I had been kidnapped and was currently rushing to a strange planet where I'd probably never be heard from again.

The alien chimes pinged, alerting me that someone was entering. More than likely, it was my friendly, sexy captor Nerisch, checking to see if I was okay. Under any other circumstances, even given that he was an alien, I might actually come to care for him. But that was not damn likely given my present setting. Anything remotely like attraction was due to the lingering effects of the sex pheromone they had dosed me with and a textbook case of Stockholm syndrome.

"Just Judith, are you ready to explore the ship today or do you plan to spend another day in here sulking?" he asked with an easy demeanor.

"That depends. Are you going to allow me to contact anyone from Earth, or perhaps the Galactic Alliance today, or will you make up another bullshit story to hide my captivity?" I responded.

He laughed, a deep, sexy, rich sound that went straight to my core. Damn, I wondered if I could come just by listening to him laugh. My brain seemed to be wired to always think about sex, even if my body wasn't craving it as intensely as before.

"I have told you the truth. Despite our ship having the most up-to-date communications systems in Orcqlaneasus's fleet, we have encountered a series of problems both sending and receiving messages," he lied.

"Yeah, right," I said, unbelieving.

"Just Judith, play nice today. Let us have no more talk about captivity and trafficking, although your imagination is quite vast," he said with a devastating green smile, a hint of fangs barely visible.

"I'm not going to let you gaslight me into believing I'm anything other than a kidnapping victim, despite your alien charm," I countered.

"Aw, you admit you find me charming. That is at least a step in the right direction," he grinned.

"How about this, why don't you let me meet with my clients, the Pstoadys?" I petitioned.

I made this request daily, and like clockwork, it always ended Nerisch's good humor with a definitive no. But today, he paused.

"If I allow you to meet with the Pstoadys, I will have to be present, and that is not up for debate," he said, surprising me yet again. I was just about to agree when he added another stipulation.

"I also want you to make more of an effort with my brethren, starting with leaving this cabin and interacting with them on the ship," he said.

"Really? I would think fucking them on alternating nights was interacting with them enough," I said sarcastically.

I knew Nerisch wouldn't like that response because we'd all come up with an uneasy truce of sorts. The estrus seemed to be in remission. I couldn't think of a better word to describe it. As long as I continued to fuck the aliens. And as strange as it was, I couldn't only fuck easygoing Nerisch. No, I had to fuck the others too, or the symptoms came back with a vengeance.

Each night I fucked either Helvich or Coervich, although fuck was probably more descriptive than what we did. Either one of the Elders would enter my stateroom and, with no comment, foreplay, or communication, he would enter said dick into said pussy. It was a very clinical, non-emotional agreement, and amazingly, both parties tended to orgasm together.

I tried to remain detached from the activity, but sadness often rolled in once the Elder left me with his nightly deposit. Nerisch would then enter and gather me in his arms. Sometimes we'd have sex after, sometimes not. Sometimes I'd cry in his arms like the first time I'd been with all of them, but that occurred less and less often now.

I knew they were breeding me, for all the good it would do, but I couldn't resist them. And though the other two would never dare to admit it, they couldn't resist me either. Our bodies were compelled to come together even if our brains and spirits were not aligned.

Nerisch shrugged and turned to exit when I called him back.

"Wait, I'll do it. I agree, I'll try to interact with your brothers beyond their nightly emissions, and you'll let me meet with the Pstoadys unencumbered," I said.

"No deal. The Pstoadys are tricky, and we' are too close to the outer boundaries of where Quadrant Three and Four intercept, to be waylaid by any of their mischief," he said. "As it is, we are not traveling at the speed we were en route to Nyokaa, with no discernable rationale."

"Assuming, of course, that you're not lying, are you implying the Pstoadys have anything to do with your shipwide problems? If so, that's even more reason for me to speak with them," I pleaded.

Nerisch crossed his arms, a clear indication he intended to be unyielding. I knew my next move had to be strategic, and maybe a little hoeish. Just like I couldn't resist them, they couldn't resist me. At least not sexually.

I walked over to him and wrapped my arms around his waist, forcing him to abandon his closed-off stance and embrace me.

Leaning into him, I said, "That's not fair at all. I've done everything you've asked of me. You could extend me a little trust. What trouble could I possibly get into by speaking with the Pstoadys?"

I felt his exhale and knew I had won this round.

"Fine. But let us start with a civil conversation with my brothers. One that does not begin or end with you calling them kidnappers, sex traffickers, abductors, handlers, or any of the myriad human terms you have used to denigrate them," he said.

Hugging him, I agreed and followed as he led me through the maze of the ship's corridors.

"How can you even find your way around here? This place is massive. I bet someone could hide out here for weeks, and you'd never know," I said.

"Maybe this was a bad idea," he said and turned to head back to my stateroom.

I rushed to grab his muscular arm. "I was only kidding. I'm sure you guys have state-of-the-art tracking and surveillance systems."

"We do," he said with finality, and we continued through the maze until we reached the bridge, the control center of the ship's operations. Noticeably present were my two late-night fuck boys—or maybe fuck aliens.

Coervich, whom I had come to realize was the absolute epitome of a walking, breathing asshole, spoke first.

"What is she doing here? It's a little early to be getting my cock sucked," he smirked.

"Leave her alone, Coervich," Helvich said dismissively, turning his back on me and returning to his duties at the command station.

"If the human wants to be fucked off-schedule, I'd be more than happy to oblige. I was looking forward to getting my dick wet tonight," Coervich laughed, insultingly.

I looked at Nerisch, who seemed to be barely holding his anger in check. But I didn't need him to come to my rescue. Rather than shy away and hide, I stood up to my mate. I wouldn't run or cower behind Nerisch. Now that I was here, I had a greater mission at stake, and I wouldn't let juvenile antics make me uncomfortable or dissuade me from my task.

"Well, if this is the way your species treats lifemates, I can definitely see why you were on the verge of extinction," I quipped.

Nothing. I was met with absolute silence. Maybe I'd hit a little too close to the truth.

Helvich turned around and looked at me. I thought I saw a hint of a smile, but if so, it was fleeting, and he turned back to his task.

Coervich looked pissed, but he didn't have shit to say after that.

Seeing an advantage, I kept the conversation going by airing my reason for entering the bridge.

"I want to see my clients and make sure they're okay," I said.

"Absolutely not," Helvich said emphatically, followed by silence from Coervich.

"I told her she could see the Pstoadys if she ventured from the stateroom and interacted more with her mates," Nerisch said.

"I interact with her as much as I am inclined to. My answer is still no. She should not be anywhere near the Pstoadys. But I am sure, brother, she will twist your dick and you will give in to her wishes regardless of what we have to say," Coervich said resentfully.

Before Nerisch could respond, I fired back.

"You act like you're my hostages rather than the other way around. You control everything, not me. There's nothing I can do unless you allow it."

I laid it out for my captors like they didn't already know the basic rules of captivity.

"Take her off the bridge. I do not care where she goes as long as it is away from here," Helvich said.

Nerisch sighed and left the bridge without another word. Not one to stay where I wasn't wanted, I quickly followed behind him.

As we walked and took an elevator to another level, I teased, "Well, that went well."

Instead of being angry, he rewarded me with his signature smirk.

Exiting the elevator, we were confronted with another maze of corridors and panel doors. Just when I was beginning to believe he was intentionally walking in circles to disorient me, we arrived at a large panel opening.

Upon entering, I saw my twin clients encased in a large glass holding cell. Although holding cell was probably not what it was called, that was the closest thing I could come up with.

It looked like a large stateroom with four walls, one of which happened to be made of glass so the occupants within could be viewed.

I walked over to the glass panel to speak with the Pstoadys, and Nerisch stopped me. He passed his clawed hand over an invisible control panel, and the glass pinged and shimmered, instantly garnering the attention of the alien inhabitants.

"Judge Judith Jiminez Jackson, we are so pleased to see you," the taller one, Torvak, said.

"Yes, we wondered if you would visit us," the other one, Tovak, continued.

"You were expecting me on the ship?" I asked, confused. Nothing was making sense. Why were the Space Orcs keeping the Pstoadys confined if they were all working together?

"Of course, Judge Judith. We leave nothing to chance," Torvak started.

"Everything is carefully planned with our subjects," Tovak continued.

"Subjects, as in test subjects?" I asked unbelievingly.

"Exactly!" they said in unison.

I was about to bring righteous hell down when the ship rocked from an explosion. The lights flickered off, and the klaxon proximity alert blared the following announcement:

"Enemy incursion imminent. Guests, please make your way to the nearest evacuation pod and await further instruction."

Nerisch's rich voice blared out over the looped emergency announcement.

"J.J., are you okay?" he asked while physically assessing if I was in fact okay or not.

"Pstoadys, are you responsible for this?" he boomed.

"No, Elder Nerisch. We are not!" they said in frightened unison.

Nerisch ran his hand over the invisible panel again and freed the Pstoadys from the glass compartment.

"Follow me back to the bridge. I need to see what is happening," he ordered.

I had a million questions, but I knew better than to ask any right now. He held my hand, and we rushed toward the elevator that had brought us to this level. All the while, the klaxon continued to blare, and the recorded A.I. loop directing guests to safety played on endlessly.

In much shorter order than it had taken us to reach the Pstoadys, we returned to the bridge.

Helvich and Coervich were no longer in their Elder robes. Instead they wore armor harnesses strapped across muscular green chests, each a distinct shade. My heart skipped a beat, because even though they might be Elder Space Orcs, the twelve packs of abs on each one gave no indication of them being past their prime.

Each of the Elders walked toward me, assessing my appearance, while Nerisch opened a compartment of battle armaments and strapped up in war gear like his brothers.

Helvich walked over to me and lifted my chin, studying me carefully.

"Are you okay, J.J.? Were you hurt in the explosion?" he asked quietly.

I was astounded. It was literally the nicest thing he had ever said to me, short of asking me to be his mate, of course.

"I'm fine. What happened?" I asked.

"We are under attack by a squadron of Gernicians," Coervich said.

"Gernicians? I thought they disappeared deep into Quadrant Two after the defeat of their benefactors, the Mesetholie, in the Distant Wars," Nerisch queried.

Each of us present was familiar with the Distant Wars that extended to all members of the Galactic Alliance, including Earth. Our colony of homesteaders on Nu-Terra had fallen during the first wave of attacks by the Mesetholie, a spiderlike species of aliens that cocooned its victims in husks to feed upon.

The galactic battle had raged for five years until the Mesetholie were eliminated like the plague they were. It was determined well into the war that the Gernicians, also members of the Galactic Alliance, had been working with the Mesetholie for years.

When Gernicians were found to have been working with Galactic Alliance enemies in the past, it was always explained away as rogue elements or terrorist cells operating outside the government. But the Distant Wars pulled the deceptive veil away, exposing the Gernicians' treachery and the many years they had engaged in horrifically brutal acts of torture.

As a presiding judge of the World Court, I had seen raw footage of the abuse and spoken to survivors of the carnage of Nu-Terra. Although the Gernicians were nothing like the threat posed by the Mesetholie, their brand of mind control, deception, and torture made them a formidable enemy.

Of course, they would attack a lone ship on the boundaries of overlapping Quadrants. I just hoped my mates would be up to the challenge. Three Elder Space Orcs against a squadron of twelve Gernician ships, each filled with a platoon of soldiers.

The comms chimed, indicating an incoming message. It was being transmitted from one of the Gernician warships circling us.

"I am of a mind to simply ignore them altogether since they have blown a hole in the side of our ship," Helvich said.

"I agree. But let us at least hear what the fuckers have to say. At the very least, it will buy us more time until reinforcements arrive," Coervich added.

"Good point," Helvich said. "Nerisch, our guests."

"On it," Nerisch said.

He turned to me and the Pstoadys. "I need you two to stay out of sight," Nerisch said.

"What about me?" I asked.

"You definitely need to stay hidden. We do not know why they fired on us. They are deceptive fucks, but this makes no sense. Even outnumbered, they should not think they are a match for us," he said.

He directed us to a small junction panel. It wasn't very big, housing a series of conduits for the ship similar to a complicated circuit breaker setup. It was just enough room for the three of us. Nerisch went to close the panel, sealing us behind it.

"Do you have to close it? Will they see us if you leave it open?" I asked.

"Leave it open, Nerisch. They should all hear what is going on. Everyone is affected by this," Helvich proclaimed.

"Coervich, open a channel and let us hear from these fuckers," Helvich said.

The screen shimmered and cleared, revealing the elongated craniums of the Gernician males. Their skin was translucent, stretched tight across bone, their pale grey eyes flat and lifeless. Each one wore a slate blue metallic bodysuit that shimmered beneath the feed's dim light.

"Orcqlaneasions, your ship has been disabled. Prepare to be boarded by the superior Gernician legion."

The lead Gernician spoke with no inflection. "Turn over the Pstoady scientists and the human, and we will offer you a merciful death."

He stared directly into the lens. "We have intercepted your transmissions. Hidden signals. Buried requests. We know what you are hiding."

Another Gernician stepped forward, his voice calm and final. "We know your secrets. But your extinction will not be rectified. Your time in this galaxy and any other is over."

The screen flickered once. Then the final line came through. "Surrender them immediately."

# CHAPTER 10: Coervich, The Mate

Gernicians. Scheming, deceptive, manipulative alien fucks. They should have been exterminated as surely as their confederates, the Mesetholie.

Since when did they have the balls to go up against Orcqlaneasions? Hell, they were not even strong enough to go up against humans.

The situation was dire. The call for aid had gone out. Orcqlaneasus Command had acknowledged, dispatching nearby brotherhoods. The Galactic Alliance replied with less urgency, more bureaucracy, but it did not matter.

All communication had been cut, solving the mystery of what the fuck had been impeding it for the last two weeks.

Shit, twelve Gernician ships surrounded us. Help would arrive too late.

I stood on the bridge, weapons locked tight around my body, pulse steady. My bound brothers, Nerisch and Helvich, flanked me.

Helvich's jaw was clenched. Nerisch, his eyes kept flicking toward our mate, the human.

She stood too close to him, as usual. I could smell her fear. Taste it on the air. And Nerisch, idiot that he was, drew strength from it.

"Focus on the battle at hand, brother," I said, just loud enough for him to hear.

"Where would my focus be, brother?" Nerisch replied, irritated and anxious for battle.

"Your obsession," I spat.

"You mean our mate. The one you have sworn to protect with your life," he said mockingly.

Helvich's eyes darted between us but he said nothing. There was no time to argue.

Normally, Nerisch would take the lead in battle. He ran endless simulations preparing for it, and preferred it over diplomacy. But he would not leave her.

"Enemy breach imminent in five, four, three, two, one," the ship's A.I. counted down, detached and calm.

In our old ship, the fuckers never would have made it this far. First, they would have had to crack the shield grid, a fluctuating algorithm designed by Orcqlaneasion engineers to be unbreakable.

Second, if by some fluke they got through, our old ship's hull was reinforced with a hybrid alloy, stronger than titanium and virtually impenetrable.

But this vessel had neither.

This ship was equipped with long-range comms and diplomatic transponders. Tools suited for negotiation, not war. The outer skin was sleek and pretty, but soft, not built for battle.

That would be rectified once we reached the homeworld. And we would reach it. I would make sure of that.

"They are not wasting time," Helvich muttered, powering up his trillium blades, one blade scraping against the other with a metallic screech.

"Good," I growled. "I want to meet them up close."

We split up. Helvich headed for the back corridors. Nerisch went to guard the Pstoadys and the female, obviously. I took the front line, just as Gernician weapons began slicing through the forward hatch.

The first soldier burst through in a blur of sleek blue metallic armor. It moved with his body, giving him agility and strength that a fragile creature like him should not have had. His most dangerous weapon was his brain, and males of their kind tended to have large heads, twice the size of their females, making it an easy target.

I fired one bolt through its head. Then I hurled my body forward, crashing into the surge that followed. I used brute force to tear through them, one after another.

More poured in, and I fought harder.

Gernicians were not strong, but this new armor upped the ante, giving them speed and coordination they did not naturally have. Two aimed for my legs while a third tried to reach my throat. I twisted, cracking two large heads against each other before turning my weapon on the incoming charge, cutting through them one after another.

The floor ran slick with blue blood. A pile of bodies stacked near the bulkhead. But they just kept coming.

Over comms, I heard Helvich grunt, then roar, then go silent.

"Nerisch?" I barked.

"Still protecting," he snapped. His voice sounded winded.

I pushed forward through the corridor, bodies crunching under my boots.

Another detachment breached the position near Nerisch. I saw them on the interior display. At least thirty, swarming toward where the Pstoadys and the human had taken cover.

"Nerisch, they are on you."

"I see them," he said. With little effort, he cut through, ending them before they ever had a chance to reach those he protected.

The female screamed, diverting our attention from the battle toward her. In an instant, Nerisch lunged in front of a plasma burst meant for the human. It struck him directly in the chest, searing flesh and dropping him instantly. He fell, grabbing her and the Pstoadys and dragging them behind the central support beam before collapsing.

Helvich and I met in the center corridor. His chest was slashed, blood seeping, but his eyes burned hot.

"I am with you," he said.

We charged. We did not speak. We did not coordinate. We simply moved, charging through innumerable Gernicians, their oily blue blood coating our hides. We were death in motion.

But it was not enough. A blade sliced my side, but I barely felt it. Nerisch was down. Our mate was unprotected. I could not lose my brother. I could not lose my mate. I fought to protect him. I fought to protect her. And I even fought to protect the annoying Pstoadys.

Helvich was in as bad shape as I was, maybe worse. But we could not stop. We would defend each other and our mate with our dying breath.

Then the floor trembled. Through the hull breach, four Warrior-class Orcqlaneasions entered the fray, offering us a moment of respite as they eliminated the waves of Gernicians that dared to attack.

From the comms, a new Orcqlaneasion voice burst through. "We will handle the ships out here. Another Orcqlaneasion vessel approaches. Do you want them inside or out?"

"Send them in. I want these blue-blood fuckers off our ship," I bellowed, using what strength I had left.

With our brothers taking the forefront and more arriving by the moment, we limped toward Nerisch.

He was barely conscious.

J.J. was beside him, crying.

The Pstoadys had stretched what looked like a security grid over his torso.

Speaking in unison, they said, "This will stabilize him. We created it on Med Base Gamma 7 when we were overrun with injured soldiers."

I nodded and slumped down beside him. Helvich dropped beside me.

"Oh my god, they're both hurt," I heard my mate say.

"Torvak, Tovak, you have to help them too. Don't let my mates die," she pleaded.

I smiled. Then I passed out.

# CHAPTER 11: J. J. Almost Home

The trip to Orcqlaneasus seemed to take forever. The Space Orcs who first arrived to help fight the Gernicians brought us aboard their ship for the journey, while another crew towed the diplomatic vessel behind us.

I was desperate to get there with my mates, which was a remarkable turn of events considering how I felt just a short time ago. Each one had been grievously wounded while fending off the hordes of Gernicians that overran the ship. I still had a hard time wrapping my head around it, and I witnessed it firsthand.

My mates had stood up to more than four hundred Gernician soldiers, killing almost two hundred before reinforcements arrived. Even the other Space Orcs were impressed by this feat, speaking about it often in hushed tones. They said it was because they had a human mate to protect—me. A fact that astounded me.

Nerisch had told me that as their mate, they'd vowed to protect me, but I never realized what that meant. Not really. Not having had anyone protect me before, it was a foreign concept. I'd always been self-sufficient back on Earth. I never sought out protection or safety, maybe because I didn't think I'd ever find it.

Loving William wasn't safe. It was wrong, impulsive, and reckless. I was young, and he was married. When things got bad, he left me to deal with the consequences alone, just like my family did when I brought William into my life. They disapproved, and instead of standing by me, they turned away.

This was different. I had accused the Orcs of all manner of horrible things, and still they protected me. I refused to go into a stasis pod, and the remedy was sexual release. Despite not wanting to be my mates, not at first, they still gave me what I needed to survive, even as I referred to them as criminal traffickers.

I misunderstood, misread, and generally got everything wrong in my dealings with the Space Orcs, with the Nyokaa, and with poor Kayla Asani, who I constantly referred to as *la bruja*. I sent her a long written message apologizing to her and her sweet little boys. I sincerely regretted calling them monsters. No wonder her mates had thrown me off their planet.

During the long journey to Orcqlaneasus, traveling at Galactic Standard, I stayed with my mates in the medical bay. Thankfully, the Pstoadys were there to render aid. I was so grateful to them for saving my mates that I forgave them, without thought, for infecting me in the first place.

***

When the ship touched down on Orcqlaneasus, I stayed close to my mates as the guards moved in. Nerisch was still unconscious but stable.

Helvich and Coervich had begun to stir, their breathing stronger and their movements less sluggish.

The Pstoadys coordinated seamlessly with the Orcqlaneasion guards to prepare the stretchers and arrange secure transport. They weren't off the hook though, not from the Directorate, and as Orcqlaneasus was a closed society, they would not be allowed to step foot on the planet. Still, they had saved my mates, Elders of the Orcqlaneasion Directorate, and I knew from a legal standpoint that might go a long way toward reducing the penalties for their prior infractions.

The ramp lowered with a low hiss, and a single figure waited at the base. It was Ambassador Vivien Johnson.

We weren't exactly close, but I knew her. We'd shared space on Earth, in courtrooms, conferences, and high-level summits. She was Earth's voice to the stars, and I was one of its judges. Although we weren't friends, we traveled in the same rarified circles of educated, professional Black women in spaces that weren't built for us, but that we had carved our way into. We respected each other and the struggle it took to get where we were.

When she saw me step off that ship, she didn't hesitate. She came straight to me and pulled me into a hug. It wasn't a diplomatic formality but a full-body, sister-to-sister embrace. The kind Black women give each other when words just aren't enough.

"I'm so glad you're here," she said, her voice full of emotion. "I heard what happened. I know you've been through a lot."

I held onto her like the gravity of this world was heavier than the last. And she let me, feeling what I felt, knowing what I knew. She was a lifeline from my past and an anchor for my future, and even though we hadn't really been friends before, I knew that we would be now.

"My niece, Dr. Nina Bridges, is waiting for you," she said. "She's been coordinating care since your signal came through. During the

Distant Wars, she and the Pstoadys saved more lives than I can count. You're in the very best place. And in the very best hands."

I nodded, swallowing the lump in my throat.

Behind me, the guards moved in synchronized silence, assisting my mates across the platform. The Pstoadys remained aboard the ship, flanked by the Orcqlaneasion warrior crew who had traveled with us. Once the transfer was complete, they all turned and disappeared back into the vessel.

As Nerisch's hover-stretcher passed by, his limp arm slid off the edge, and I reached to place it back across his chest. The guards, seeing my gesture, paused in reverence as I pressed a kiss to his fevered brow, wondering when he had managed to burrow his way into my heart.

"They're being taken to one of our protected recovery wings," Vivien added. "We'll take you there now."

"Thank you," I said quietly.

She gave a small nod, and her voice softened even more.

"You're not alone anymore, J.J. Whatever happens now, you've got people here for you."

For the first time in a long time, I let myself believe that might be true.

***

By the second week, Nerisch opened his eyes.

He didn't speak at first. His gaze drifted across the room before settling on me. I sat upright in my own pod nearby, awake, watching him.

His brow furrowed like he was trying to piece together the timeline. Then his fingers twitched."I'm still here," I said, not moving. "We're all here."

He blinked slowly like the words took a moment to sink in. He tried to speak but only exhaled. I didn't need him to say anything. Just seeing his eyes open again was enough.

His injury had been severe. If it hadn't been for the cutting edge medical technology the Pstoadys used to stabilize him, he would have succumbed to it within minutes of being shot.

Dr. Nina told us his recovery would take the longest because of the nature of his wound. It would be a long and arduous process, but there was every expectation that he would recover.

Helvich had regained full consciousness a week earlier. I heard him before I saw him, arguing with the mechanical med-bot that was adjusting his neural stabilizer. He slapped the scanner away, then sat upright and scowled in my direction. When he realized I wasn't going to respond, he just stared for a while before giving a short nod.

He wanted to be up and back in control, but his body still needed to heal. He stayed in the medical bay, reluctantly, while the slow recovery continued.

Coervich came around after that. He was still closed off, still observing. His eyes followed me whenever I crossed the room. One day he asked for water. I brought it without a word. He took it without a thank you. That was progress for us.

I knew he held me responsible for Nerisch's nearly fatal wound, and he was right. It was my fault. If I hadn't screamed and distracted him, he wouldn't have been injured.

I'd been assigned my own healing pod across the bay from theirs, close enough to monitor but far enough to give space. I didn't sleep with any of them. I didn't even sit near them unless one of them stirred or reached. I gave them room to recover on their own terms. But I stayed.

I stayed through the recalibrations, the muscle reconditioning, and even the awkward, wordless meals. There was a silence between us that lingered. It wasn't hostile, but it wasn't easy either. It was a space we hadn't yet figured out how to fill.

By the end of the month, Nina's scans showed full stabilization. Nerisch still moved slower than usual, but he could stand. Helvich paced in the med bay unit like a tiger in a cage. Coervich, who by my estimation seemed completely healed, observed and stalked. He watched everything and said nothing.

The silence continued, and without Nerisch fully healed and fully present, I didn't expect warmth from them. And I wasn't wrong.

***

With my mates' recovery on track, I was worried when Dr. Nina entered our medical unit and asked to see me. I'd avoided getting checked out when we came in because I hadn't been hurt, and my primary concern had been my mates. I didn't want time or resources wasted on me with my mates barely hanging on to life.

"I know you said you're okay, but with everyone on the mend, I'm planning on releasing you all in the next couple days. But before I do, I need to confirm my diagnosis," she said.

"What diagnosis? Is our mate ill?" Coervich said, surprising everyone except maybe Dr. Nina.

"No, no, I realize now what I've just said might have sounded cryptic. Nothing's wrong. I just need to scan J.J. to make sure everything is fine."

She indicated that I should lie down on my medical bed and pulled the scanner arm down, running it across my torso. Images appeared on the vid screen attached to the monitor.

She turned the screen toward me without a word and smiled. Even though it looked different because of the alien technology, I knew an ultrasound when I saw one. And when I saw the pulsing heartbeats glowing on the screen, I was overcome with emotion.

"What is that?" I asked, even though I already knew.

"You're pregnant," she said. "About eight weeks along."

I stared at the screen, looking at and listening to the strong heartbeats.

"Conception occurred just before the Gernician attack," she added. "Most likely a couple days prior. The monitor shows four strong fetal heartbeats."

I had assumed they were breeding me from the start. That was the whole point, wasn't it? I had called them monsters for it. Had told myself I was nothing but a vessel. But I never thought anything would take. Not after everything that happened on Earth. Not after all the loss. All the pain.

"I don't understand. I'm postmenopause. I can't be pregnant. I'm too old and too weak," I said between tears.

I felt strong arms embrace me, and I pulled away. I didn't want Nerisch to exert himself lending me comfort, but it wasn't him holding me. It was Coervich.

Knowing it was him, feeling sorry for me, made it all somehow worse.

My mind couldn't really process it, and it broke me. I started to cry, uncontrollable tears that would not cease.

I heard Dr. Nina trying to console me, but it didn't work. It was like I was in a fog, a bad dream I couldn't shake myself out of. I couldn't be pregnant, not again, not at my age and not by these males.

They deserved someone whole. They deserved a family and sons, something that I couldn't give them.

They had fought to protect me, risking their lives against insurmountable odds, suffering injuries and painful recovery. And I wasn't worth it. I couldn't give them what they wanted, what their society needed. I was the weak link. And just like before, the passion would turn to disgust, leaving me more broken than before. I didn't have that much loss, that much sorrow within me.

I heard voices around me, but I couldn't make them out. I was lost in my grief for my past and my future.

I felt the familiar sting of a hypospray, and slowly, I drifted to sleep.

# CHAPTER 12: Nerisch, The Mate

I was frustrated with my slow recovery, especially knowing how much J.J. needed me.

She was not the same, and we could not reach her. My brethren tried to comfort her, but they did not understand her, having never tried to before.

I was a warrior in elder garb, and this situation confounded me. I thought: if this were a campaign, a battle, how would I approach it? Suddenly, I knew the way forward. I needed my brethren.

I approached Helvich and Coervich in the garden of our new dwelling, assigned to us by the Chief Elder upon our release from the medical unit.

To call it a garden was perhaps an overstatement. It was overgrown and offered direct entry into the vast tropics of our homeworld. If it were up to me, I would leave it in its natural state. But that surely meant my brothers would want to change it. Still, this was a small problem compared to our much bigger one.

"Brothers, I would like to speak to you about our mate," I said.

"Now you choose to speak to us about our mate? Where was that consideration when you decided for us to take a mate, brother?" Helvich said, surprising me.

"Do not mind him. He is angry that we cannot reach her," Coervich said, surprising me with his insight.

"I agree. She is slipping away from us. I will tell you what I know of her past, which may provide a clue. J.J. had a previous life partner, but he died in years past. The scars on her belly, the ones that appear as faint stripes, indicate when she carried a life in her womb, more than once. Each time, the child died, and she still grieves their loss. I believe this is the cause of her sorrow," I said in explanation to my brethren.

"Why would you keep this information from us? When did you learn of this?" Helvich said.

"I hid nothing from you, brothers. The truth of what I speak is etched on her body. If you had taken the time to notice, you would have seen it too instead of rutting her like an Andrenian stallion," I said.

Helvich returned my barb with an answering growl, to which I responded in kind. This battle with my brother, always at odds, had simmered for annums, and I was prepared.

"Enough," Coervich yelled. "We have no time for a brother brawl because you say right and you say left, leaving me to determine which course of action is correct."

I laughed. "You would choose Helvich's direction after deliberation, of course. But still, you would decide a course, and I would follow as a bound brother should, without question or pause."

"I made the choice to give us a mate. A life beyond our diplomatic white robes, settling disputes until our minds and bodies gave way. I chose to give us a chance to be fathers, to have sons, to cherish a human female. And all you have done is resist at every turn."

Coervich walked toward me and placed his claw on my shoulder. "You are right, brother, especially in choosing our mate. Even if we did not trust her, we should have trusted you, our brother."

I placed my claw on his shoulder, and Helvich walked forth.

"I regret my words and actions, brother. You were wise in choosing a mate for us."

He placed one claw on my shoulder and the other on Coervich's. We each returned the gesture, forming a triad, claw to claw, a symbol of the sacred bond we took so many annums ago.

Releasing our claws, we still had to solve our most pressing problem, our inconsolable mate.

As if reading my mind, Helvich said, "We must determine how to help J.J."

"I agree," I said. "We know very little of her life before coming to us."

"Precisely, brother. We need to learn more of her background to find the root cause of her malady," Coervich said.

"Earth Mother Evalynne Browne, the mate of the Chief Elder and his brethren, was an investigator on her planet. She may be able to get us the information we need about J.J.'s past to help her," Helvich said.

We were united in our cause with no dissension, for the first time in annums, for her.

***

We met with Elders Fraebrion, Maer, Rektrion, Bryll, and Earth Mother Evalynne Browne at their residence two weeks later. Chief

Elder Illbrien Rezz had attempted to attend the meeting but was ultimately unable to adjust his schedule. He had repeatedly set and changed dates and times until a final arrangement was made without him.

Elder Fraebrion welcomed us into their home. Seeing him alive and thriving was disconcerting after believing he had perished after the death of his twin brother years ago. His brother and I had been friends when we were younglings, well before we were bonded. In truth, I had thought I would be bonded to both Draebrion and Fraebrion. However, the Elders had chosen another pair and a different path for me.

"Old friend," Elder Fraebrion said, placing his claws on my shoulder. I returned the gesture, sensing the surprise from my brethren at this unexpected reunion.

"I am pleased to see you alive and well, my friend. I believe you met my bond brothers several annums ago. Helvich and Coervich," I said.

My brothers nodded in greeting, and Fraebrion reintroduced Rektrion, whom we had also encountered during past peacekeeping missions as warriors.

Earth Mother Evalynne Browne entered carrying a white-haired hybrid toddler.

She walked toward Elder Rektrion, who was smiling. "I give up. He won't go to sleep like his brothers, and I'm tired of fighting with him."

Elder Rektrion chuckled. "Just like his sire. He knows when something is going on and is far too alert to sleep through it. He will settle once he sees our guests."

Evalynne glanced toward us. "You should have brought your mate. Seeing the little ones is comforting when you're carrying one of your own." She patted her belly and smiled.

"Congratulations," I said warmly.

"Our sons shall be great friends," Rektrion declared, causing everyone to laugh.

"We are here about our mate. We know little of her past, and learning she carries our sons has caused sorrow rather than joy. We wish to understand her time on Earth, to learn how to help her," Coervich said.

"Hmmm, digging into someone's past is a heavy request. Are you sure? You might not like what I find. Some secrets are better left undiscovered," Evalynne replied.

"We are in agreement. Our mate has shut down, and nothing else has worked," Helvich said.

"I can find out what you want, but trust me when I say this. Going behind her back to get information, even if you think it's for her own good, will backfire. It will more than likely make things worse, not better. I'm a woman, a Black woman, and I'm telling you this from personal experience," she advised.

Heeding her words was not easy. I knew my brothers would be unsettled by this sudden change in course the Earth Mother had counseled. I braced for another round of debate, only for Helvich to speak first.

"I hope I speak for my brethren when I say we will trust you in this matter, Earth Mother Evalynne. If you believe the course we follow is unwise, we will cease immediately. We do not wish to cause our mate further distress. We only wish to alleviate her current dismay," he said.

I meant to respond, but no words came. My tongue was still, stunned by my brother's immediate acquiescence. I turned to Coervich, who gave a steady nod, and without hesitation, I did the same.

"Good, trust me when I tell you, your mate will appreciate that you let her share her past on her own terms. You just need to have patience," she said. Then, shifting the conversation, she added, "By the way, thank you for finally bringing in the Pstoadys."

"The Pstoadys have become a bigger problem now that they are in custody," Rektrion said.

"Half the planet sees them as saviors. The other half views them as enemies of the state," Fraebrion added.

"In any case, the Pstoadys cannot be allowed to roam freely, causing havoc for unsuspecting humans and Orcqlaneasions. Even if they mean well, as so many seem to think," Evalynne said.

"Although I wouldn't trade my life now for anything, the path they set us on was so harrowing we barely survived," she continued.

"Your experience and the recent battle are further consequences of their meddling," she added.

"While I agree the Pstoadys have set many unintended events in motion, I cannot blame them for the rise of the Gernicians. That fault lies with the Orcqlaneasion Directorate. At the behest of the Galactic Alliance, we allowed the Gernicians to scurry into hiding after the Distant Wars instead of eradicating their entire existence," Helvich said.

"In that, brother, we are in agreement," said Chief Elder Illbrien Rezz, striding into the formal salon of his residence.

My brethren and I were surprised by his appearance. His family seemed less affected, all but his small son.

The toddler reached out to Chief Elder Illbrien, who held out his arms, and leapt into his sire's embrace.

Speaking to his son, Elder Illbrien said, "You are supposed to be napping like your brothers. I am disappointed, son."

The toddler began to cry. Elder Fraebrion stood, retrieved the child, and quietly exited the room.

"Duties kept me away. But it is my understanding that you are here to ask my mate to obtain information about yours. I agree that would be ill-advised," Illbrien said.

"I'm not going to ask, at least not here in front of our guests, how you know that considering you weren't present. But we will be having a conversation, Illbrien," Evalynne said.

"Yes, brother," Rektrion added. "That's far more information than you could have gotten from our bond alone."

The Chief Elder smiled and nodded, deftly sidestepping the accusation.

"I am indebted to you for bringing in the Pstoadys. However my family can help yours, we will. They are currently under guard on our alpha moon, awaiting trial. They have insisted that your mate represent them. But given her current condition, I chose not to inform her."

I felt and heard my brethren growl at the high-handed way the Chief Elder had made decisions on our mate's behalf. Before any of us could speak, his mate responded angrily.

"That wasn't your call to make, Illbrien. Giving J.J. the chance to work on an intergalactic legal proceeding might be exactly what she needs. It's something familiar, something she's good at. Being an older woman, pregnant on an alien planet with mates she barely knows, has left her feeling out of control. That is the opposite of who she is. She was a judge on the World Court," Evalynne said.

"You are absolutely right, beloved. I overstepped," Chief Illbrien said, shocking everyone. "Brothers, I apologize for the callous way I've handled this. Speak with your mate, and if she chooses to represent the Pstoadys, we will move forward accordingly."

"Thank you, Chief Elder. We will relay the message, and our mate will contact you with her decision," Helvich said.

"Yes, and thank you, Earth Mother Evalynne for your guidance and insight," I added, eager to return to our mate armed with this new information.

If what Evalynne said was true, we might finally have a solution. Perhaps acting once again as legal counsel for the Pstoadys might be the spark J.J. needed to awaken from her malaise.

# CHAPTER 13: J. J. A Place Called Home

It's funny how no matter how different things look on the surface, just beneath, they stay the same.

When I was pregnant before, I'd stay in bed for the first three months, hoping it would make a difference. Dr. Nina said I was fine, that the babies were strong, but I didn't believe her. I knew my body. I doubted I could carry alien children any more than I had human ones. Still, I followed the only routine I knew. I stayed in bed, isolated for the first trimester. Or, in this case, the first quarter, since alien pregnancies lasted twelve months instead of nine.

But I'd made it. The first quarter had passed, and I waited anxiously for Dr. Nina to confirm what I barely dared to hope.

As if summoned, she stepped into my room with Helvich.

"Hello, J.J. How are you feeling today?"

"Today, I'm great, and I really hope that I can get out of bed and start moving around a bit," I said.

Dr. Nina glanced at Helvich, then back at me.

"I think you'll be able to be more active. Let's check on the babies."

She pulled out the portable scanner and hooked it up to the vid screen. Unlike before, this scan looked like a real ultrasound.

"Now that they're bigger, you'll see them in a way that feels familiar. This is similar to a 5D ultrasound back home," she said.

She kept talking, but I wasn't listening. I saw my boys, clear and strong, for the first time. Tears ran down my face as I reached for Helvich's clawed hand.

"Where are…" I started, but Coervich and Nerisch rushed in before I could finish. They crowded around me. My eyes were on the babies, but their eyes were on me.

"*Mira eso... mis bebés están bien*. Look at our sons," I said, nudging their focus. Each one glanced at the screen, then turned back to me.

"J.J., I know it's hard to believe they're okay, but they are. And I don't want you staying in bed the whole pregnancy. That could do more harm than good. This is a hybrid pregnancy. It won't follow the same rules," she said.

"I understand. It's just, I lost so much. Five beautiful souls, all gone." My voice broke. I couldn't say more.

"I know you didn't want to go to the healing ponds before, but now I'm insisting. Once you're there, you'll feel the babies, really feel them. You'll know they're safe," she said.

She powered down the scanner and unplugged it from the screen. I took each of my mates' clawed hands and placed them on my belly.

"Talk it over with them. I'll send the coordinates."

Taking a deep breath, I asked a question that, in any other circumstance, might have made me expire from sheer mortification.

"Do we really have to have sex in the pond, together?"

"Absolutely, you make your offering, and Laneasus grants you and the babies health. It may also help your mates," she added.

"I am fine, Dr. Nina. My concerns are only for my mate and sons," Nerisch said.

"Of course you are, with no lingering effects at all from receiving a near mortal wound," she said with her usual dry wit.

She checked her wrist communicator. "Aerix is here for me. I told him this would be a short visit. Let me know when you return from the healing ponds, although you won't need me again after that until it's time to deliver."

She waved a quick goodbye and turned to leave. Nerisch stood from my bed and ushered her out to her mate, leaving me with Coervich and Helvich.

"The doctor has brought good news today, and much for you to think about," Helvich said.

"I know," I said hesitantly. Even though everything appeared normal on the ultrasound, I knew how many things could go wrong.

Nerisch returned and sat on the bed next to me, with my other two mates taking similar positions. I knew they were up to something. They hadn't all been with me at the same time since the ship, before the Gernician attack.

"What's going on?" I asked.

"We have news we need to share with you about your clients, the Pstoadys," Helvich said.

"The Pstoadys? I can't represent them any longer. My first priority is my babies," I said.

"It seems Chief Illbrien was right after all. I do not look forward to letting him know," Coervich said.

"The Chief Elder stated you were not fit to represent them due to your current indisposition. We disagreed with his decision to speak on your behalf, but perhaps he saw more than we realized," Helvich added.

"My indisposition? Did he really say that?" I asked, incredulous. Typical. A male assuming that pregnancy somehow made me incompetent.

The Pstoadys' case was relatively simple. It boiled down to a series of miscommunications between species. There was no malice, no premeditated harm. At every step, they believed they were following the guidance of Dr. Nina Bridges. She'd told me as much during my time in the med-bay while I waited anxiously for my mates to recover.

I'd used that time to reach out to the other humans as well. Each one had sent me a brief account of their experiences with the Pstoadys. Once Nerisch and the others began recovering, I found out I was pregnant and put everything on hold. But I could do this.

"Dr. Nina and Vivien believe that the healing ponds will strengthen the pregnancy and assure me of its viability. I know I've been making all the decisions about the babies, but I don't want to do it alone anymore. Each of us is going to be a parent. So, we should all decide together whether we go there or not," I said, my voice halting.

Helvich took my hands in his clawed ones.

"I have been a poor mate to you, and for that, I make no excuses. As a warrior, I once dared to dream of finding a mate. But as each annum bled into the next, it became impossible. I accepted my role as Elder diplomat without question or regret. Your very existence shifted everything I believed and understood. I chose not to trust what my eyes saw clearly. Having you as my mate is my greatest joy, though I do not deserve it. I vow to protect you, to share my lifeforce, and to cherish you for all my remaining days. You carry our sons, but I would choose you a thousand times over, with or without the promise of legacy."

Tears flowed freely down my cheeks. During my confinement, each of my mates had spent time with me separately, giving me the space to truly know them. Of all of them, I knew Helvich the least. Words didn't come easily between us, but still, he came every day. The long silences, once awkward, became comforting. I missed him when he was gone. And now, these words, the most he had ever spoken to me, bound me to him once again as his mate. Words were still difficult, but I nodded quickly and hugged him, pressing my face to his warm, solid chest.

"Being of a similar mind as my bound brother has never annoyed me more than in this moment," Coervich growled, temporarily breaking the bond between Helvich and me as we both laughed at his scowl.

"My brother delved into my thoughts and wrenched the words I planned to say to you for himself," he complained.

"I didn't think the bond worked like that," I said.

"It does not. It is more a sense or feeling, similar to human intuition but much stronger," Nerisch said.

"I know I have been an asshole, siding with Helvich instead of following my own mind, and I deeply regret that. As Helvich expressed using my thoughts, I vow to protect you, to cherish you, to share my lifeforce and seed with you for all my days," Coervich grumbled.

"We are, at long last, united in our desire to be your mate. Will you accompany us to the healing waters of Laneasus, for our sons, our bond, and our family?" Nerisch asked.

"I will," I said, feeling a sense of joy and relief for the first time since I began my odyssey with the Space Orcs.

"Good, Nerisch, get the transport ready. Helvich, carry our mate. I'll make sure we have the coordinates from Earth Mother Nina," Coervich said, issuing each directive in quick succession.

"Wait, we're going right now?" I asked, caught off guard by how fast things were moving. Before anyone responded, I was already being lifted into Helvich's arms and swept out of the room.

Moments later, I was aboard the waiting hovercraft.

***

We reached our section of the healing waters in no time, making me wonder if my mates had planned this journey in advance. I pushed that thought to the back of my mind, since I was much too nervous about our upcoming shared intimacy in the healing waters.

My mates, on the other hand, had no such worries. They quickly disrobed and entered the waters, leaving me standing in my hesitation at the water's edge.

I told myself this was safe. They were my safe place. I repeated it over and over again as I looked at each of them, at the new scars they'd earned to protect me, risking their very lives for mine.

I pulled off my nightgown and underwear and stepped into the small lake.

Nerisch approached me first, which made the most sense. He lifted me in his strong arms, and his lips met mine in a passionate kiss. I missed the feel of him, the press of his lips on mine, and my body knew it.

I felt the heat of another press behind me as claws captured my breasts. Lost in the kiss and the tingle of sharp fingertips dragging over my skin, I barely noticed when Nerisch reclined against the lake's sandy edge, still kissing me.

I wrapped my legs around his thick torso, my body hot like it had been in the early days of my heat, before they succeeded in getting me pregnant. My pussy clenched from the memory, and like a magnet, his dick pulled at me. I sank down, encasing him deep, every inch locked inside me in one slick slide.

Nerisch plunged inside, stretching me wide and filling me completely. I screamed my pleasure in this alien landscape becoming one with my mate.

I turned my head and saw Helvich, his thick dick glistening with pre-cum. Eagerly, I swiped my tongue across it and moaned at the rich, minty flavor. He pressed the spearhead into my mouth, further and further until it was wedged in my throat. It was raw, brutal, and alien and I was overcome with sensation.

Nerisch pummeled my pussy and Helvich fucked my throat. My body shook over and over, climaxing beneath the overwhelming ferocity of being claimed by my alien mates.

I didn't think it could get more intense until I felt Coervich behind me. His claws dragged slowly down my back before he gripped my hips, spreading me open with deliberate force. Then I felt the blunt pressure of his dick at my ass. I had never taken anyone there. I had never even thought about it. Especially not someone with a dick that thick.

But Dr. Nina and the others said the pheromones made us compatible. That our bodies adapted. That we were remade to take them fully, every inch, every time.

I didn't know if that was true, but in that moment, I believed it. I felt it. My body was ready, made for this, made for them.

The thrill of surrender, fullness, and the unknown sent another orgasm crashing through me before he even breached me. I tore my lips off Helvich's dick just to scream. Then Coervich pushed forward and buried his whole fucking pole inside me. My ass stretched wide around him, my body shocked by the pressure and the pain and the pleasure all at once.

I was breathless, panting and needy. I moaned again and Helvich resumed his place in my throat. I was full, each of my mates fucking me without mercy, the heat of their skin and the strength of their bodies making me theirs in every possible way. Our bond locked into place. We were united as one in body and spirit.

We came together with my body pulsing, milking them as they emptied themselves inside me in perfect synchronicity.

Helvich pulled back first, letting his dick slip from my swollen throat. Coervich followed, dragging out of my ass with a slow, delicious sting. Nerisch stayed the longest, grinding once more into my pussy, holding me to him before growling and finally letting me go.

I collapsed, boneless and dazed, draped across Nerisch's chest, held safe in their arms.

A mist rose from the lake, thick and heavy like a fog. It covered all of us, wrapping around my belly and breasts and winding around the torsos of my mates. It disappeared as quickly as it came, leaving the waters clear and undisturbed as though we had never been there.

I felt a sense of peace I could not explain. My babies were okay. Better than that, they were whole, and they were going to make it. I was connected to them in a way I could not explain. I was also connected to my mates, and I knew the blood sacrifices they had made for me in the battle with the Gernicians had been honored with a full and complete healing.

We exited the lake quietly and reverently, each of us with our own thoughts. All of us aligned, ready to return home and take our place in the life we had fought to keep. The sacred waters would call us again, but not for healing. Next time, we would return for the birth of our sons.

This wasn't the fairytale ending I ever imagined for myself. But you know how I felt about fairytales. What I had was real. It was built on the trust I had to earn, the fear I had to face, and the safety I never thought I would find. Standing there with my mates beside me and our children growing inside me, I knew one thing for certain.

There was still a happily ever after.

And this one was mine.

# EPILOGUE: A Room With A View

*A small vid-screen captured the interplay of subjects on the bridge, unbeknownst to them, of course, as two small Pstoady scientists watched and listened intently from their glass-enclosed holding cell.*

"It's inconceivable to me that those two little scientists caused this much trouble," Whorvek said.

"I know, especially since our entire peacekeeping force has been looking for them," Chozek replied.

"To be fair, they were hiding out on Nyokaa. Who could have anticipated that, especially since our own brothers sent them there," Shavrek said quietly from his place on the bridge.

"Yeah, but think about what brothers sent them," Whorvek continued. "Those four are barely warriors at all. They've never followed the code, even as young warriors. They're bloodthirsty assassins through and through."

"And somehow they have a mate," Chozek said. "A human mate and sons. Incredible."

"Yes, it is incredible," Whorvek said. "Those four are the least worthy of continuing their lineage and with a beautiful human."

"She is beautiful, lush and fecund. I'm at a loss as to how they are deserving," Chozek marveled.

Ghorvik entered the bridge and looked to his brother. "I sense frustration, Shavrek. Has news been relayed from the Directorate about our alien guests?"

"No, what you're feeling is the mewling whines of your brothers, ever complaining about their lack of mate," Shavrek replied.

"No, brother. We were not whining about not having a mate, rather questioning why Laneasus would honor the treachery of the assassin-kind with both a mate and sons," Whorvek explained.

"Not that again. Since we've returned to Orcqlaneasus the only two topics of conversation are: are the alien scientists heroes or criminals and how our brother warriors, not assassins, earned the right to a mate and sons," Ghorvik said in exasperation.

"It seems hours of fruitless debate suits you well, brother, as we inch closer to elder class from warrior class. I would however be more concerned about the rise of the Gernicians, especially in their show of force against our diplomats," Shavrek said.

"They must have thought Elder Orcqlaneasions would be no match for them. In truth, who could have imagined that three Elders could hold off a squadron of twelve ships single-handedly?" Chozek asked.

"It was because of their mate," Shavrek said flatly.

A pinging chime indicated an incoming message transmission from Orcqlaneasus.

"Finally, news from Orcqlaneasus. Let us hope they have finally set a trial for our guests so that we can return to our patrol sector in Quadrant 4," Ghorvik said.

"That's if we can return to our old sector. With the advent of the families on our planet and the new threat of attacks by aliens as weak as Gernicians, I wonder if we will be tasked with returning to our previous mission," Shavrek mused.

As the vid image shimmered to life on-screen, the presence of Chief Elder Illbrien Rezz, Orenik Cyradis, and Helvich Dralvion appeared.

"We've received an urgent request from the Galactic Alliance, relaying a distress call from an interspecies xenoanthropological team stationed on the planet Mars," Chief Illbrien said.

"That was the sector you were assigned to before answering the call to return to Orcqlaneasus, was it not?" Elder Helvich inquired.

"It was. But we shut down all expeditions on Mars before we left. We planned to install a planetary security grid to keep intruders off the planet before returning to Orcqlaneasus, but we were interrupted when we received the distress call from Elder Helvich and his brethren," Ghorvik grumbled.

"That would explain how the team of intergalactic researchers made their way onto the planet, but not why Gernicians would attack a destitute, barren planet," Orenik said. "I have a bad feeling about this. Illbrien, do you have a record of the species comprising the research team?"

"I do. I'll pull it up now," Chief Illbrien said. Displaying the roster on-screen for all to see, he added, "Shit, I see it. That must be what they're after."

"Undoubtedly. Going to Earth would be too dangerous for them, as well as its moon. Finding a lone human female amongst a team of alien scientists on an isolated planet without a security detail in place is too ripe of a qwizi for them to pass by," Elder Helvich said, referencing the sweet fruit all young Orcqlaneasions loved, despite its toxic outer shell.

"My adopted niece, whom you refer to as Earth Mother Lydia, has been working on increasing the speed of ships traveling at Galactic Standard. Her fleet of prototypes is housed not far from your location on Moon Alpha. Get to her shipyard, and one of her mates will set you up with the fastest and most agile one. "Unfortunately, I must warn you, what you make up for in speed, you will lose in weaponry. A bug, as she calls it, that she is still working on," Orenik said.

"We will leave now and place the Pstoadys under the jurisdiction of our brothers, Earth Mother Lydia's mates," Ghorvik said.

"No. Take the Pstoadys with you. Their advanced medical technology is second to none. Depending on what you find on the planet, their help might be invaluable," Chief Elder Illbrien said, surprising all with his words.

"Don't the Pstoadys pose a risk to the human?" Shavrek said, just over Ghorvik's shoulder.

"They do. But I've come to believe their primary mission is to protect the lives of humans and Orcqlaneasions, especially after the assistance they rendered with our brother Helvich and his bound brothers. It's a risk I'm willing to take," Illbrien said.

***

"We are needed," said Torvak.

"Yes, we are needed," said Tovak.

"I am afraid of the Gernicians," said Torvak.

"As am I," said Tovak.

"The Space Orcs will protect us," said Torvak.

"Yes, just as they have always protected us," said Tovak.

"We will help them, too," said Torvak.

"Yes, we will help them find a mate," said Tovak.

"Yes, they long for a mate and sons, like their Space Orc brothers," said Torvak.

"Yes, like all Space Orcs, they long for a mate and sons," said Tovak.

SOLAR BLACK

# SPACE ORCS AND THE PROFESSOR

THE LAST OF THE ORCQLANEASIONS

# SPACE ORCS AND THE PROFESSOR

## THE LAST OF THE ORCQLANEASIONS

# CHAPTER 1: Angela's Story

The first day of school was always stressful for me. Whether I was a student or on the other side, as I was now, that groggy, nauseous feeling, like everything was going to go wrong, never quite went away.

I knew what I should have done to get over it. I should have gone to the club like I used to back in the old days. Nothing quite hit the spot like a hard pounding from an anonymous dick. But fuck, old was the operative word. Once I hit fifty, finding a good dick attached to anything remotely in my age category was Missionary Impossible, I thought with a laugh.

Maybe I should have popped a couple of Xanax with a chaser of Trazodone. That always was the preferred cocktail at my local neighborhood psych unit, but since I'd been stable for the last seventy-five months without one 'discernible episode' better not to dredge up that shit.

Fuck, I lost my train of thought. Oh yeah, I felt like shit. Never did I imagine that I'd still be preparing for school all these years later, but at least now I was the educator, not the student. Not that I minded. Chronic depression aside, some days I loved the life I'd carved out for myself. Today just wasn't one of them.

"Damn," I said out loud to no one in particular. I saw the heads of a couple of undergrads turn in my direction. Freshmen, no doubt, judging by the way they ambled through the hallway cautiously, looking at one door and then the next. I laughed to myself.

I hustled to find my room assignment, desperately trying to make up the time I'd lost fighting first-day traffic. They kept trying me with my placement every year, shuffling my room assignments more than once over the summer. I honestly thought they were trying to rage-bait me into going off on somebody, hoping I'd crash out. Yeah, I'd done it in the past, but it hadn't helped my career and had almost cost me my tenure.

Pushing those thoughts down with the others, nervous excitement prodded me forward as I found my way to 3313, this semester's home for ANC1701, Advanced Studies in Ancient Alien Civilizations.

I pushed open the door, only to be met with the uncomfortable realization that I'd stepped directly into the middle of a class already in full session. At first, I felt like the wandering freshmen I'd seen moments earlier, stepping into the wrong classroom, but that was quickly dismissed when I saw the sea of puzzled faces staring back at me. It took me a few seconds to register the lecturer, who'd stopped speaking as I entered the room.

"Oh, Professor Thomas," my colleague said, seemingly undisturbed by my interruption.

I couldn't believe what I was seeing. What the absolute fuck. Why was this asshole in my assigned lecture hall? I took a deep breath and thought about my options. I wanted to cuss this bitch-ass man out. Short term, I knew it would make me feel a hell of a lot better, but was it really the best thing to do in the long run? Yeah, I had my shit together. Look at me, reasoning through my anger. Plus, I knew that any untoward "rage" behavior on my part would have this fucking place Baker Acting me with all deliberate speed. I should know, since they'd done it before, and on more than one occasion. So I took the high road, stifled my agitation, and made it look like I was contrite.

"I'm sorry for the disruption, Dr. Menard. My schedule lists this room for my course, ANC1701," I said quietly, hoping to minimize the anger bubbling beneath the surface.

Contrarily, Menard's voice boomed throughout the room. "There's no need to apologize, Professor. This is ANC1701. There was a flurry of last-minute changes. Knowing your penchant for paper communication, you probably missed them," he said condescendingly.

"I received no notice of this change," I replied, keeping my voice level. "Not by email, not through the registrar, not in writing."

He was so typical of most of my colleagues that it would have been comical if I wasn't so angry. White male—check. Man-bun—check. Scruffy beard—check. Skinny—check. Arrogant—check. Privileged—check. Asshole—check, check, check.

While running through my assessment of him in my head, he pushed a new paper schedule into my hand.

"This should help you out," he said, then turned back to my students, now his, and began lecturing while I stood there, trying to process what was written on the document.

I couldn't believe what I was seeing. Fueled by this new insult, I found my feet and left the lecture hall. Once the door had closed behind me, I reread the new schedule Dr. Menard had given me.

ANC1701: Due to increased enrollment, an additional section of ANC1701 has been opened in a virtual format to accommodate student interest in the course. Please report to Grant Hall for your new cubicle assignment.

This was impossible. What the fuck were they playing at now? Were these people really trying to goad me into some type of episode? Fuck, my paranoia was off the chain. Was it working? Was I being paranoid, or was this some shit they'd conspired to throw me off my game?

I couldn't understand. Why would I be assigned a virtual section when I clearly had more experience and accolades than Menard? Hell, I was the reason students signed up for the class in the first place.

Grant Hall was where adjunct professors taught online courses from windowless, soundproof cubicles. It was located on the lower floors of the facilities building, and since the building housed the university's servers, it was always cold and sterile. It was, quite simply, the basement, the place where careers went to die.

Yeah, they had me all the way twisted if they thought I was going out like that. Without thinking, I found myself walking not toward Grant Hall but toward my department chair's office. This had to be a mistake.

On the short walk to Dr. Dickerson's office, I used every stress-mitigating strategy I knew to calm down while I tried to figure out what to say. Yeah, I had issues, but it's not like I was a slimy predator like some of my peers, pushing up on their undergrads even though they were old enough to be their fathers. Those fucks had actually been promoted. How had my career suddenly nose-dived to the university's basement?

Dickerson was cut from the same cloth as my other colleagues, with one notable exception. His attempt at a man-bun was more or less a comb-over, his dusty white hair pulled conspicuously over his obvious bald spot.

I'd watched with humor over the years as he'd aged horribly right in front of my eyes. Maybe I should've been kinder, since he'd been the first person to offer me a job after my incident nearly thirty years ago. He'd also kept me employed as he moved up the university's political ladder to his current position. Still, I never really liked the man, and for all his fake concern, I felt like he really didn't like me either.

After all, it was his signature on the documents that put me in a seventy-two-hour psych hold when shit fell apart. Maybe I shouldn't have blamed him when those 'initial observations' lasted for upwards of six months to a year. Plus, it took another six to nine months to slowly get weaned off the heavy meds they put me on. It was a fucked-up cycle, but it wasn't really his fault. Sometimes I just lost my shit.

But today that wasn't going to happen. I wasn't about to let anything or anyone flush seventy-five months of sanity down the toilet.

Reaching his office, I noticed it was unusually quiet, especially for the first day of classes. Generally, there was a hubbub of activity from the day's events. I wondered where everyone could be.

"Dr. Thomas, what are you doing here?"

The question came from Dr. Dickerson's personal secretary, Maggie, a middle-aged white woman who wore her clothes a couple of sizes tighter than necessary.

"I'm looking for Dr. Dickerson," I said.

"Everyone is in the conference room. Your old mentor has an announcement. Didn't you read the memo?" she said breathlessly.

Again, I thought just a little more room in those clothes would go a long way toward making her sound less asthmatic. And what was the deal with me supposedly not getting messages? This was starting to piss me off.

I followed Maggie into the conference room, which was more like a small auditorium the way it was set up. I was met by a sea of curious white faces looking at me like I didn't fucking belong. Seriously, I'd been here longer, been published more, had better ratings, and ran circles around their mediocre asses. Before my eyes could locate Dickerson in the crowd, the wall-sized monitor vibrated to life.

Somehow, I found a seat as the room dimmed and all attention was directed to the screen. It was a good thing, because when I saw Ryan's face on the screen, my whole world stopped.

My anger dissipated. My chest tightened. I felt sweat seeping from my pores. I ran out of breath. I was having a full-blown panic attack. The timing was awful, happening in the midst of my colleagues. The strategies I'd learned from years of hospitalizations and countless therapy sessions disintegrated like dust through my fingers as quickly as I grasped them.

I couldn't let everyone see me fall apart. I couldn't let them validate all the rumors about me. I could dissolve later, in the relative comfort of my own home, away from everyone.

I put that place in my mind, a place of peace and tranquility. My home was my sanctuary. I'd curated every corner of it to bring me calm when my thoughts were stormy. I let my mind drift there, to my expansive garden. I saw the antique white gazebo. In my mind it was in full bloom. Roses in pink, purple, and red climbed the trellis. Lavender lined the walkway. Marigolds and daisies filled the beds near the fence. Hydrangeas stood heavy and full. I was there, not here. From that vantage point, I could breathe in the sweet scent of flora surrounding me, and the words I heard from the voice I knew so well were diminished, not nearly as harsh or brutal as they had been in real life.

They were still untrue, always the most beautifully crafted lies draped over the most rotting, decaying, obvious truths. I'd been so young, so needy, so fucking eager.

In the darkness of the room, the memories exploded before my eyes.

***

*"It's so exciting," I said. "I can't believe it's actually true."*

*"Right, right, pull up the last paper," Ryan barked, bustling with nervous energy and reflecting my excitement.*

*"Our research, what we put together will be the foundation of communication for first contact with the alien species and the government," he said, with a twinkle in his ice blue eyes.*

*Of course I knew this. I'd read the email like everyone else. In addition to being a research assistant to Dr. Ryan Murphy, I handled all the communication for the research team he headed up.*

*I pulled up the files on the iMac with Dr. Ryan (that's what I called him) pressed against my shoulder, so close it made me all kinds of giddy. While skimming the paper, an email notification pinged, and he touched me again, this time pushing my hand from the mouse, sending sparks of something as his fingers brushed mine.*

*It was a secure government document, but he struggled to open the file.*

*"Here, I can get in. Let me do it," I said, familiar with his access codes and flustered by his closeness.*

*The official letter from the U.S. Space Force was littered with legalese, most of it about liability and responsibility, but once we waded through that, we saw the real intent of the message.*

*"Dr. Ryan Murphy, you and your research team have been commissioned to participate in an interspace mission to meet with members of the alien species currently in orbit in our galaxy. Your team will travel via shuttle in the next seventy-two hours to our base of operations on the moon."*

*I read it aloud to Dr. Ryan as the others crowded around to hear the news. It was the best outcome for the hard work we had put into mapping out a communications structure in the unlikely event of meeting alien species.*

*Our research had been obscure and often ridiculed. Yet once it was confirmed with undeniable proof that life existed beyond Earth, our team went from being educational pariahs to the most sought-after researchers in all academia.*

*Initially, we weren't even a team. Dr. Ryan, Perez, Brett, and I had all been contacted separately by an envoy from NASA and the Space Force. Brett had come from the East Coast, while Perez came from the West. Dr. Ryan and I were Florida natives, but from completely different worlds. He was Palm Beach old money, and I was Fort Lauderdale, no money.*

*We were tasked to work together and provide insight on the alien species that had made first contact with humans. Dr. Ryan became our leader, forming us into a team. He treated each of us with respect and admired our skill sets.*

*Perez was a programming dynamo. He created intricate code to find connections virtually invisible to the human mind. Brett took all the data and made it make sense, creating trails for us to follow, linking morphemes and graphemes that would eventually lead to acquiring the basics of language decoding.*

*My gift was understanding it. Once the raw data was released to me, it was like a game of Sudoku with no answer key. The only other person on my team with similar skill was Dr. Ryan, and even he wasn't able to make the connections to the language the way I did. But Ryan was humble, never taking credit for anything I uncovered as we worked in lockstep to unravel the code and make alien languages comprehensible.*

*As we re-read the message flickering on the iMac, each of us slowly realized what it would mean for our future.*

*Perez was the first one to speak. "This is fucking unbelievable, fuck yes," he said, jumping around unexpectedly. He was slight but still muscular, with a face so smooth it looked like it had never seen a razor, which made him seem younger than he actually was. He was super pale, and whenever he tried to tan, he would come to work the next day looking like a lobster. I guess he was cute, but I didn't go for white boys, not unless you counted Dr. Ryan, because I definitely had a crush on him. His outburst was funny because he was generally pretty shy and spent most of his time locked away in a small cubicle near the servers, happily creating code that only he understood.*

*Brett was another story altogether. He knew everything, or at least that's what he seemed to think. There was no subject he wasn't an immediate expert on, outside of his actual realm of expertise in data disaggregation. Whether it was the optimal temperature to grow roses or the moontide's regulation of a woman's period, Brett could deliver a full-throated argument on any subject. He was constantly giving unsolicited advice on the best way to do this or that, which made him difficult to be around at times. Like most of the men of science in my sphere, he was of average height, maybe five-eight, lanky with mousy brown hair generally pushed behind his ears, frameless glasses perched on the bridge of his nose. He wasn't bad-looking, but the know-it-all energy was a lot. And white boys didn't really do it for me, with one notable exception.*

*Compared to the other men on the team, though, Dr. Ryan was a Hollywood glamour boy. In real life he was probably a six or seven, but by academia standards he was a ten-plus. A lot of the female undergrads gave me envious glares with whispers of how lucky I was to be his grad assistant, which I mostly ignored. At first his All-American blond-haired, blue-eyed look did nothing for me, but he was charismatic as well as smart, and eventually I was hanging on his every word like everybody else.*

*His looks and charm bought him a lot of goodwill from everyone, the university's president, the dean, hell, even the head custodian yucked it up with him. He was the epitome of privilege, the youngest of five sons from a wealthy Catholic old-money family. I couldn't imagine a person more different from me, but somehow the thought of him did something to me.*

*I was a plus-size nerdy girl from the Sistrunk side of Fort Lauderdale, Florida, and even though I was currently without a man, my usual go-to were the big, buff brothers from around the neighborhood. Sadly, those dudes usually got with girls far more interested in hair and makeup than I could ever be. In fact, my beautician was a barber, and I kept a nice low-boy fade, because who had time to be bothered with hair? Research mattered. Unlocking the code to communicate with alien species was all-consuming, and only the men in this room shared my zeal, my determination to succeed.*

*Dr. Ryan brought some semblance of composure back to the happy discord. "Okay, everybody, I know we're excited. This is what we've been working toward, to be rewarded like this. All I can say is this is a lifetime achievement, and I couldn't be happier sharing it with each of you."*

*"Let's celebrate," Brett said excitedly.*

*"That's a great idea," Perez added.*

***

My memory started going fuzzy then. I was jolted back to reality, sitting in the back of a darkened conference room. I saw Ryan's face in vivid high definition on the wall-sized conference screen. My palms were sweating, and I felt myself once again hurtling toward that panic attack. I squeezed and unsqueezed the arms of the chair I was sitting in, shutting my eyes to keep the rush of disjointed memories at bay.

Breathe in. Blow out. Hold for three seconds. Breathe in. Blow out. Hold for three seconds. No one could see me losing my shit, I thought, but I pushed that thought away too. I could do it. I'd done it before. I was strong. I had my shit together now. Breathe in. Blow out. Hold for three seconds.

I wasn't sure how long I focused on my breathing, but I felt more than saw when the lights came back on. I was once again composed. Well, at least composed for me.

Our department chairman was speaking when I re-engaged with reality, and I hoped I hadn't missed too much. Hell, who was I kidding? I'd missed every fucking thing. I prayed that he would recap whatever Ryan had said, and fortunately he did.

"I want to reiterate the government's position on this as relayed by Dr. Murphy. Anyone participating in the unsanctioned alien archaeological mission on Mars will be terminated immediately. You will not be able to share or publish your research findings, nor will you be employable by any institution of higher learning, be it public or private," he said gravely.

A murmur of assent went through those assembled. Meanwhile, I was taking it all in. Did he really say there was an unsanctioned archaeological dig going to happen on Mars?

Dr. Dickerson continued, "If you are contacted by a private entity attempting to enlist you in this endeavor, you must contact me immediately so that we can alert the authorities. As you know, as members of the Galactic Alliance, we benefit from both the technology and defense of the organization, and participating in this campaign would be a breach worthy of an intergalactic incident. Although we were not directly touched by the recent Distant Wars, we lost our first colony, and the death toll of alien allies numbered in the millions, with several species across the galaxy involved."

Now that I was on the same page as everyone else, I understood the gravity of the situation. My mind was still racing, but my inner turmoil was invisible on the outside. Dr. Dickerson answered a few questions, and everyone started to leave. My virtual course mix-up would have to wait, since I was in no condition to have that conversation. I hoped to slip out unnoticed, but of course, no such luck.

"Dr. Thomas, I'd like a word, please, before you leave."

Damn, he caught me. All I could do was nod and stop in my tracks. I glanced around anxiously as the room cleared and the department chairman spoke to others in the department before finally bestowing his attention on me.

"I'm glad you came to today's presentation. I was afraid you wouldn't attend," he said.

"Well, of course I would attend. This is quite significant," I said, trying to muster the gravitas needed for this conversation.

"Yes, Dr. Murphy wanted me to reach out to you directly, since he feels, as do I, that you will probably be contacted about this expedition," he said, watching me intently.

"Me? I'm probably the last person on Earth who would be contacted," I said.

"Everyone associated with Dr. Murphy and his research team will be at the top of the list. Have you been contacted by any entity about this expedition?" he asked.

"No. This is the first I've heard of it," I said.

Dr. Dickerson stared at me as if trying to decide whether I was telling the truth. He nodded and gave himself a small shake, almost as though dismissing the idea that I would be contacted. After all, I hadn't gone on that first pivotal mission when we'd made contact with the aliens from across the galaxy, and sadly, everyone knew why.

He turned his back to leave, letting me know the conversation was over. Before exiting, however, he said, "Be sure to let me know if you are contacted," repeating his earlier request.

"Definitely. But I doubt I'll be contacted," I said.

***

After the meeting in the conference room, I was still too unsettled to do anything but seek the comfort of my home, so I took off early.

My house was my safe space. When I first bought it with the settlement money two decades ago, it was just a rundown Key West style bungalow in Fort Lauderdale, with its only saving grace being its proximity to the Atlantic Ocean. Layer by layer, I uncovered its regal beauty, replacing old wood, scraping and painting. I brought it back to life, and in doing so, I healed from the trauma of a painful attack that stole my future and almost ended my life.

As I approached my porch, I noticed a package. That seemed a little curious, but since I shopped online pretty frequently, I figured something had arrived that I'd forgotten about.

I brought the package inside and set my purse and briefcase on the small table in the hallway. I kicked off my shoes and went to the wine fridge. A cool glass of iced Moscato was exactly what I needed to take the edge off, and since it was low in alcohol content, it wouldn't mess with my anxiety meds.

I took a sip and remembered the package. For the life of me, I couldn't remember what I'd ordered. I picked up the small parcel, carried it to the sofa, and sat down. I set my Moscato on the side table and tore open the package.

Inside was a small rectangular box. I opened it. Nestled on top was a brand-new phone with a note that read, "Please power on this mobile device."

Okay, I definitely hadn't bought a phone, but maybe it was some kind of promotion. I powered it on, only to realize it wasn't a phone at all. It was an intergalactic communication device, humming softly with a faint green glow once it activated.

I was holding it and staring at it in awe when the personalized message began.

"Greetings, Dr. Angela Marian Thomas. We would like to offer you the opportunity of a lifetime."

I smiled, thankful for today's briefing. This was the call I never thought I'd get. This was my second chance, no, my last chance, twenty-eight years later, but still another chance to participate in an alien archaeological exploration on Mars.

Fuck the government, the Galactic Alliance, Dickerson, and especially Murphy. I was definitely going this time and nothing on Earth would stop me.

# CHAPTER 2: Whorvek Vandri - Space Orc

"What do you mean we do not have a plasma cannon on board? Every basic Orcqlaneasion ship has at least one as standard equipment. Even transport shuttles have them. They are fucking standard issue," Ghorvik boomed.

Meeting Ghorvik's anger with slow, measured words, Shavrek responded, "I have run the weapons check more than once, and it is not there. We left Orcqlaneasus in such short order, there was no time to conduct a complete weapons check."

"No time to run a weapons check? Are you insane?" Ghorvik asked incredulously.

Chozek entered the bridge while Ghorvik was bellowing, took in the scene, and slumped into his station at navigation. Meanwhile,

Shavrek stood to his full height, immediately challenging the anger in Ghorvik's words.

"At what point were we supposed to stop and run a full systems check of this ship?" Shavrek asked with flagging restraint. "We all heard the order to leave at the same time. Based on our last encounter with the Gernicians, with an attack imminent on our previous post that was left unsecured, there was no choice but to take the fastest ship and leave," Shavrek countered.

I had hoped that Ghorvik missed the quick missile Shavrek fired about leaving the sector Mars inhabited unguarded, without a security grid deterrent. Ghorvik had given the order and was directly responsible for the consequences of that action.

As our numbers decreased over the centuries, our technology improved to keep other species from invading our homeworld. We had engineered a nearly perfect security grid that had never failed, until, of course, the incident at Nu-Terra that incited the disastrous Distant Wars and decimated our numbers even further.

Judging by the low growl coming from Ghorvik, he had not missed the jibe. And it did not help that Chozek, in typical Chozek fashion, was grinning like an idiot while observing the tense exchange between his bound brothers. Ghorvik's growl deepened in intensity as he made his displeasure known, taking a battle stance toward our brother. Before Shavrek could return the gesture, Chozek glibly made an announcement.

"Approaching Mars space in five, four, three, two…" he said. "Shall we put an end to this altercation, brothers, and see to the business at hand? But if battle is what you are after, I detect four Gernician ships hiding just behind the larger moon, Phobos, and two more shadowed by the smaller moon, Deimos."

"Fuck!" Ghorvik boomed.

Instantly, the anger dissipated between my brothers like the early morning fog at dawn's break on Orcqlaneasus. Each brother took his station. Ghorvik took his place in the captain's chair, Shavrek took the helm, I checked the comms, and Chozek resumed his position at navigation.

Without thinking, I asked out loud, "How did we end up here this fucking fast?" Realizing what I had just verbalized, I said aloud, "Shit!"

"Exactly, brother. This fucking ship!" Ghorvik bellowed. "Chozek, run a scan of the planet for any life forms. Helm, put those moons on the vid screen. I want to see where these fuckers are hiding."

Each of us knew our tasks, fine-tuned over decades of working together in lockstep. Hearing the words was more a mantra than a command.

Our mission was urgent, but rushing could cause deadly mistakes. I knew this. My brethren knew this. Hell, every Orcqlaneasion knew this.

We had left our homeworld at breakneck speed, traveling in the foreign new ship provided to us by Earth Mother, Lydia Collins. Although the ship was untested in battle, we were not, and given the mission at hand, we were all in, even Chozek, who gave an outward appearance of detached lassitude.

The vid screen soon filled with the image of Mars's two moons, the smaller and the larger. Chozek enhanced the image, making it clear to see the six other ships partially obscured by each of the moons.

"Well, we know where they are. That is a plus. I would wager they are hiding, waiting for Orcqlaneasus to come to the party," Chozek said, a hint of humor in his voice.

"There is no way they would be expecting us here this soon. They knew this sector was unguarded. That is why they targeted it. Maybe we should fall back and find out what they are doing," I suggested.

"Normally, I would agree with you. That is the most solid plan, but I am not willing to take any chances if there is really a human female on that planet. We do not have a choice," Ghorvik said.

Shavrek offered a solution, putting his recent altercation behind him. "We have a couple of shuttles on board, and they each appear to be equipped with the 'bells and whistles' we were told about."

"Bells and whistles?" I asked, completely confused. Why the fuck would we need either of those on a ship dispatched for rescue or battle?

Chozek spoke to clarify the situation."Humans have a way of saying something without saying anything at all. 'Bells and whistles' refers to additional enhancements to the ship. While you were securing our Pstoady guests for travel, Earth Mother Lydia and her mates went over the upgrades with us."

Ghorvik asked impatiently, "What do we have, brothers? I focused more on what was missing, like the lack of armament."

"The ship has the latest Multi-Adaptive Stealth Technology, or M.A.S.T. Each shuttle and the ship are equipped with the technology," Shavrek said.

I had a vague recollection of what it was, but before I could ask, Shavrek, picking up on my befuddlement through our brotherhood bond, provided more details.

"M.A.S.T. is a stealth technology that allows our ship to remain undetected, both visually and by short-range sensors," he tersely explained.

Hearing what it was, I had even more questions. Stealth technology was extremely rare, even among members of the Galactic Alliance. As far as I knew, only Nyokan ships carried the technology, and those snaky aliens were not likely to share it.

"Veltrufh Grend, one of Earth Mother Lydia's mates, shared with me the details of the acquisition of this new technology. Apparently, the Nyoka royal family felt responsible for not providing an adequate guard for the Orcqlaneasion diplomats, their human mate, J.J. Jackson, and the two Pstoady scientists in their custody. Dukari Asani, at the request of his mate, Kayla Asani, provided the technology specifically to benefit the females of Earth should they be in jeopardy or duress," Shavrek explained.

"Well, if we have this technology, we should put it to use," I said, admiringly.

Chozek spoke confidently. "Way ahead of you, brother. The ship has been in stealth mode since we entered Mars space. That is how we have such a keen vantage point on them right now. We can see every move they make, and they do not even know we are here."

I set aside my annoyance at not being informed about the capabilities of our ship. Communications specialist was but one of my roles on the ship and in our brotherhood. I thrived on strategizing and planning. That meant, of course, that I needed to know everything at all times to put the best plan into effect. While I had been trying to glean any information I could on our Pstoady guests, I had missed a treasure trove of information that could ensure a positive outcome to our mission.

"Brothers, is there any other information that I am not aware of? Any small detail could make the difference between failure and success," I said directly, my frustration thinly veiled.

"As you have said, brother, the speed of this mission has us at a disadvantage. We trust you, Whorvek, to create a sound plan that we will implement without delay," Ghorvik said, allaying the tension on the bridge. He continued, "Chozek, what have your scans found? Is the human female on the planet?"

As I listened, my mind began to play out various scenarios for my brethren and me to find and rescue the human female. Should a battle ensue, I would have to account for the lack of firepower we were accustomed to. The M.A.S.T., however, outfitted on both the ship and shuttles, provided more opportunities if it proved reliable. There were too many unknown variables that could sway the outcome, and not in our favor.

Hearing the steel in Chozek's voice caused me to focus solely on his words.

"There are several life signs on the planet's surface, most of them Gernician. I am initializing the satellites we left in orbit to map out the security grid system and scan the planet's surface," he said.

Left unsaid, but felt by all, was that if we had simply installed the security grid before leaving, this eventuality would never have occurred. The Gernicians had forced our claws then by attacking our Elder diplomats, and once again now.

Images sharpened as the vid screen focused and refocused, giving us a skyline view of three Gernician ships and a retrofitted salvage freighter on Mars's surface. Moving in closer, we could see the bodies of five other alien species scattered across the unforgiving planet. Two were Gernician, one male and one female, obvious by the size of their craniums. There were two Tekaari, most likely the security team based on their size and the demolished weaponry around them, and a molted Avian.

"That looks to be the unsanctioned scientific mission team rotting on the surface, with the exception of the human," Shavrek said.

Thankfully, the human female was not among the carnage, and it was reassuring not to see her body decaying among the others.

"Chozek, search for the human's bio-signature and tag her location," Ghorvik ordered.

Quietly, we waited, certain of our brother's ability to find her. In moments, our faith in him was rewarded.

"I have located her, buried in the collapsed lava tubes of Mars's underground cavern system. Based on human physiology, she is deteriorating. We have less than ten minutes to reach her. Her heart rate is unstable, and her blood pressure is approaching non-survivable levels. Human death is imminent without immediate intervention."

Fuck, we had been complaining about the speed required for this mission, but without it, the human would already be dead. I put those thoughts aside and constructed a plan to share with my brethren.

"Brothers, we have two options, strength or stealth. Normally, I would recommend the former. Destroy the Gernicians on the ground with our superior fighting acumen, plasma cannon or not. This would undoubtedly rouse the other ships hidden in the shadows of Phobos and Deimos. "Unquestionably, we would defeat them, but much like a buzzing neonix, with more sting than venom, the effort would take time we can ill afford. The human is near death and in need of immediate aid."

"Stealth is what is called for in this instance," I said, gaining the approval of my brethren. Looking at Chozek, I continued delivering my plan.

"Chozek and I will use the shuttle in M.A.S.T. and land on the surface, away from the Gernicians. I have determined another access point that we can detonate through and make our way to the lava tubes that still have structural integrity. It will take time, but as long as we are undetected, we will be well within the parameters for a successful extraction."

"Assuming nothing goes wrong, brother," Chozek voiced all our thoughts aloud.

"That is why our brethren will remain on the ship. They will create a distraction unique to Mars and its environment that will not be questioned," I said.

Immediately, my brothers understood the plan in detail, having surveyed the planet in preparation for the security grid installation and mapped its geological patterns.

"A local, controlled dust storm. This plan has merit, brother. We shall create a series of storms to force the Gernicians to shelter within their ships. They will not detect our presence and will have no cause to believe it is anything other than a commonplace planetary event," Shavrek said.

The strategy was sound. The time, however, was still short.

***

Chozek landed our shuttle at the agreed-upon coordinates, in a canyon formed by collapsed lava tubes millennia ago. The area was porous and spongelike, which meant it would facilitate entry to our destination. I checked my chronometer, which gave me the precise coordinates of the human's life signature, along with a programmed second-by-second countdown of the time when rescue would be futile.

I was a patient male, yet it seemed an eternity as we waited for the signal from our brethren to commence our rescue.

A signal beeped on each of our chronometers, indicating the first dust storm had begun. We would need to place small explosives to breach the cavern walls and start our descent toward the distressed human.

Another pulse from the chronometers indicated that another dust storm had formed. Using this to our advantage, we detonated the explosives and crashed through the first level of the collapsed lava tube. We were closer, but she was still too far away. It would be a race to reach her before time ran out.

Heedless to injury to ourselves, we pushed forward. Using our laser swords, we burrowed deeper and deeper within the bowels of the labyrinth of hollowed-out tunnels formed generations before by volcanic lava that flowed beneath the surface.

With claws, swords, and brute strength, we cleared the wreckage that encased the human female's body.

"Brother, the life signature has faded. I fear we have failed," Chozek said mournfully.

I refused to listen. She had to live. I would not let her die. Somehow, the mission to rescue this human had become personal. I had not seen her, did not know her, but her life meant more to me than my own.

Crashing through the last barriers, we reached the area where her life signature had been. Chozek was right. The signal had faded, but I refused to give up hope.

As we looked around, we saw nothing. The area was flat, smooth, and undisturbed. Had she been there at all?

"This makes no sense," Chozek said. "She should be here."

The chronometer signaled another dust storm created by my brethren. This one was the first of three, disguising our return trip back to the shuttle with our human passenger.

The plan I had created, executed by my brothers with precision, was all for nothing. There was no human here.

In frustration, I growled deeply and lashed out, pummeling the cavern walls. The loss I felt at losing something I had never had was incomprehensible. The grief I felt was amplified through our bond by my brethren.

Chozek gave in to his rage, his growl matching my own, but instead of lashing out with his claws at the walls of the cavern, he stomped and roared, mirroring our shared pain.

My thoughts were unmoored. I was not the calm, logical strategist my brothers depended on or needed. I forced my mind to still, to take final stock of the situation and prepare to exit. It was too late to find her alive, but if we could find her and return her to her people, perhaps there would be some solace in that end.

"Chozek, I have failed in finding the human alive. Each of us will check the final readings of our chronometers and see if we can locate her body."

"The fault is not yours solely. We have all failed in this mission," Chozek countered.

He reached out his arm, as did I, and claw to claw, we attempted to make peace with this deep loss.

Suddenly, the ground gave way, and my brother and I tumbled through loose regolith and compacted dirt for at least twenty meters, landing on something hard and familiar, like a stasis pod, but different, organic.

"Fuck," Chozek said, clambering to his feet. "Is that a human stasis pod? Why would they put her in that?" he asked.

There was only one reason. This was a trap, and we had walked right into it. Before I could get the words out, a message came through our personal comms.

"It is a fucking Gernician trap. We are surrounded," Ghorvik said. "Get the human and get the fuck off this planet. We are going to try and keep them off you. I do not think they have detected your presence in the lava tubes."

The wooden pod was unfamiliar to us. There was no digital control panel to open it. I looked to my brother. Strength was required, but we needed to proceed with both speed and caution, in the unlikely event the human was not dead.

After what felt like a millennium, we completed the task and were able to pry the pod apart using the collective strength of our claws.

The lid gave way, and the pod revealed its inhabitant.

She was beautiful. Still in repose. My heart mourned, my brethren echoed my pain.

And then, she coughed.

# CHAPTER 3: Angela Awakens

Air, I could breathe. I wasn't going to die. Well, not yet anyway.

I started coughing from the rush of air that burned as it coated my lungs. Everything hurt. My body was one big ache. Even my eyelashes hurt, or maybe it was my eyes. They felt swollen shut, and trying too hard to open them made me nauseous, adding another layer of agony to my latest near-death experience.

Why was I alive? I shouldn't be.

The last thing I clearly remembered was the bird-like alien, Fumch, pressing a hypospray into my stomach.

Fuck memories. I knew from previous experience that the more you tried to gather them, the more they slipped away, like mist through your fingers. You could feel it. You knew it was there. But you couldn't hold onto it.

My thoughts were interrupted when I heard the deepest, most gravelly voice, one that seemed to shake the earth around me.

"Human, you are injured. My brothers and I will render aid, but first we must depart immediately."

I knew it was an alien voice, and given my recent experience with aliens, I should've been terrified. I wasn't. I was in too much pain to do anything but grunt my assent.

I felt arms around me, lifting me, and I screamed, or at least I tried to. It came out more like a whimper, and for a moment, everything went black. But I wouldn't let it. I clawed my way back to consciousness, no matter how painful. I was done with pieces of memories wrapping around me like the mummified artifacts I'd been hunting.

Forcing my eyes open, I could see through the slits shades of vivid green, like Royal Palm fronds guarding my yard. But that's where the comparison ended, even to my misery-filled mind. What I was looking at was power made flesh, a Space Orc. And it wasn't just the one holding me. There was another one, too.

Both of them were tall and massive, with jet-black dreadlocks threaded with bands of white. Their bright green skin, the first thing that had caught my attention, was scarred over rippling muscles and abs etched in stone. I'd seen them on vid screens before, showcased as peacekeepers and heroes during the Distant Wars, but up close, they looked like marble statues come to life.

Whatever had happened to me must have put me in deep shit, because the Space Orcs didn't just make appearances unless it was some kind of galaxy-wide catastrophe. Thinking on it, it did make sense, because me being here in this fucked-up state was nothing short of an intergalactic shit show of epic proportions.

As my mind marveled over how my broken body had come to be rescued by Space Orcs, their communication device pinged, and I heard more thick, raspy voices.

"Brothers, we have deployed the other shuttle for the Gernicians to follow. You have got about ninety seconds to get airborne before they figure out our ruse," the voice said.

Ninety seconds. That sounded impossible, and I felt my nerves ramp into overdrive, the fear of dying or being left behind again clawing at me.

As if sensing my fear, the Space Orc's deep voice lent me comfort.

"Hold on tight, human. You are safe now. I am Chozek. This is my brother Whorvek. My brothers and I will care for you once we are on our ship."

I reached up to place my arms around him, but it hurt too much, and I slumped against him instead. He cradled me in his arms and took off running at an inhuman speed. I stopped struggling to see through my swollen lids and shut my eyes again, this time to keep my stomach settled at the unnatural pace he set.

I heard gravel shift and rocks crash as the Space Orcs ascended through the lava tubes from the underbelly of Mars. Deep down, a part of me grieved the loss of my chance to exhume the lost secrets of this alien world, but I'd come to understand soon after arriving on Mars that it was never the plan. Nothing was as it seemed, and as my alien rescuers rushed me toward their ship, I realized that I'd cheated death not once, but twice in my life.

I must have passed out again, because when I came to, we were almost out of the caves. They had told me their names, but I was fading in and out. I wasn't sure who was who, so I made my best guess. Whorvek placed an alien oxygen mask over my face, and Chozek slipped me into a foil-metallic sleeping bag.

At first, I tried to push them both away, but who the hell was I kidding? I couldn't have fought them off even at full strength. I reasoned that they wouldn't want to hurt me now, not after digging me out and rushing me back to their ship.

Chozek sought to reassure me just as I stopped struggling. "This will protect you from the elements once we leave the caverns. We will be on our shuttle momentarily, and you will be free of this place."

Being away from the planet sounded great. Chozek picked me back up, and we exited the caves onto Mars's hellscape surface. Squinting at my surroundings, I was grateful they'd put me in the alien potato sack to keep me safe.

I wondered how they were going to survive, but honestly, I knew nothing about Space Orc physiology, and I was too worn out to speculate.

I didn't see their shuttle, but fortunately, they did. In a matter of moments, we were all inside. Both Space Orcs hovered around me, placing me in the medical bay of their shuttle.

I heard the shipwide intercom chime and the voice of another distant Space Orc.

"Brothers, we see you are on the shuttle. We are setting off our final diversion, but it may or may not work, since they are aware of our presence now. You have about fifteen seconds to get airborne. Head for the friendly satellite, and we will collect you there," the voice said.

Fifteen seconds was no time, especially with both of them hovering over me instead of flying the ship. I pulled up every reserve of strength I had.

"Go, get us off this damn planet. Check on me later," I said. My voice sounded weak to my own ears. More forcefully, I tried again. "I don't want to die here. Get me off this fucking planet!"

I probably wasn't any louder, but the strength of my conviction spurred them into action. Chozek sealed the medical pod around me, and he and Whorvek rushed toward the shuttle's bridge. I felt the small ship lift off and let out a sigh of relief.

I was in pain, half-dead, on a strange alien ship, but I was alive.

As I lay in the healing pod, drifting in and out of consciousness, I tried to recall the events that had brought me to this moment.

***

*I'd never been off-planet before, so an intergalactic interview on the moon was something I still couldn't quite believe. Nervously, I kept touching the spot behind my ear where I'd gotten the translation device before departing Earth.*

*Hell yeah, I'd responded to the message to embark on an unsanctioned exploratory dig on Mars, and I could give two shits about the warnings from Dickerson or any of the others. It's not like they ever had my back. To be honest, I'd rebuilt my life from the wreckage Ryan and the others left behind, while they got all the acclaim for the work I did.*

*Not fucking happening again.*

*Since first contact, the moon had been the designated outpost for alien commerce and diplomacy, far enough from Earth to keep the public calm. So here I was, sitting in a recreation of a twentieth-century Parisian café operated by short, baby-blue aliens with small, antler-like protrusions on their heads. It was all too surreal, and I couldn't stop smiling.*

*"Is there anything else you require, Miss?" the alien server asked.*

*Startled by their sudden appearance, I was momentarily taken aback.*

*"Oh no, I'm fine for now. I'm waiting on someone," I said, but the alien walked away before I finished speaking.*

*Well damn. Rude much? I mean, I was from South Florida, where rude was an everyday occurrence, but that was just stank. Even though I was trained as a cultural xenoanthropologist, it was still hard to wrap my mind around the peculiarities and mannerisms of alien beings.*

*"Dr. Thomas, we are sorry to have kept you waiting. You have not been here too long, have you?"*

*I glanced up from my teacup, completely unprepared to see an Avian. I tried not to gawk with my mouth open, because I'd only ever seen them in vids. He, and I could safely assume it was a he, unlike the androgynous servers at this establishment, was about six feet tall with a goose-like head. He had white and brown feathers and bird-like claws instead of fingers.*

*He wore a long, leather-like brown trench coat over a brown, houndstooth, old-fashioned three-piece suit, without shoes, of course, since he had claws, or maybe talons, for feet. I couldn't say for sure since I only glanced down casually. I didn't want to get caught staring like some clueless human.*

*More amazing were his two companions. Each one was really tall. If I had to guess, I'd say close to seven feet. They were exactly what I imagined were-creatures would be if they were real. One was a cross between a wolf and a bear, and the other had the same wolfish vibe but with more of a polar bear build. They both had piercings in their ears, snouts, and above their eyes.*

*Like the Avian, they wore leather-looking clothes, but that's where the comparison ended. While the birdman looked like a steampunk aristocrat, these two looked like the extraterrestrial version of an outlaw biker gang.*

*To say they were menacing was an understatement. I almost dropped my teacup, and I noticed that every being in the establishment had gone dead quiet. Belatedly, I realized that all three of them were staring at me, waiting on my response. Damn, what was the question again?*

*"No," I said, finally finding my voice. "My shuttle came in this morning, and I've just been exploring the shops, getting acclimated to being off-planet."*

*"That is very well done," he said, shaking his goose-like head. "These are my associates, Xenon and Kytiel. I am Minister Renan Fumch."*

*He then gave me what appeared to be an old-fashioned bow. "If you would, please accompany us back to our shuttle so that we may go over the logistics of our exploration offer and determine if it meets with your approval."*

*Wait, what? My spidey senses were tingling. No way should I go anywhere with these alien beings. No matter how obsequiously polite the birdman was, the other two seemed dangerous. I'd faced dangerous men before who looked far more benign and had barely lived through it. Wow, where did that thought come from, or was it a memory? Now was not the time for my fuzzy memory to kick in, unless it was warning me about something.*

*Sensing my anxiety, Minister Renan Fumch immediately deferred. "Have I offended you in some way? I must remember that humans lack the capacity for trust. We are sorry to have taken your time. We shall depart forthwith. Of course, we will remunerate you for your time and expense. Perhaps you can take the afternoon shuttle back to Earth, and your life will not have been disrupted in the least."*

*He delivered the quick monologue in a rush, and again I was taken off guard. Ignoring the small voice inside that told me to run like hell to the nearest exit, I made a rash decision, one I hoped I wouldn't regret.*

*"No, no, I will go. I just didn't realize. I thought the meeting would take place here," I said, trying to sound more confident than I felt.*

*"Here? Of course not. The security alone is wanting. As a Minister from one of the seven royal houses of my homeworld, I only feel a modicum of safety here due to the accompaniment of my two guards."*

*Maybe I'd misread the whole situation after all. I did have trust issues. Would I let that stand in the way of my dream of space exploration?*

*I stood up and attempted to settle my bill with the little blue people. The Avian waved my hand away, so I figured he must have a line of credit or something with the establishment.*

*In any event, I left with the aliens. They had a large hovercraft that took us to the moon's enclosed port bay. There were a few ships there, but one stood out. It was a grand Gernician freighter. It was easy to tell since, just like the aliens, it appeared almost translucent from afar. It wasn't until you were near it that you could see it was made of metal, or the alien equivalent of metal, like all other alien ships.*

*Nervously, I approached the ramp that extended from the ship's hatch. I walked inside, and it was as alien and beautiful as I could have imagined. I was just taking in the gleaming blue metallic surfaces when I saw the Gernicians.*

*One was male and the other female. It was easy to tell, since the male's head was twice the size of the female's. I tried not to stare at their bodies, but with them being translucent, I couldn't help myself.*

*"Is that it? Is that the human female they desire?" the female Gernician said.*

*Minister Fumch responded, "Yes, she meets all the specifications."*

*I looked from one to the other, not understanding the direction of the conversation.*

*The male Gernician entered the confusing exchange. "It seems we overestimated the Orcqlaneasion proclivities. If this is an example of the creature they would debase themselves with, they were never worthy of our females."*

*I still didn't know what the hell they were talking about, but I got the distinct feeling that I was being dissed right to my face.*

*"Excuse me, is there something wrong? What's going on?" I asked, trying to figure out what I'd walked into.*

*Completely ignoring me, the male Gernician responded to the Avian instead.*

*"Handle that thing. The sooner we get it on Mars, the faster they'll come looking for it."*

*My arms were grabbed by the polar-bear-looking bodyguard. I pulled and tried to get away from him when the other one grabbed my shirt and ripped it open, leaving me exposed in only my bra.*

*The Gernician female took another shot at me. "It's corpulent and disgusting. Get rid of it!" she said in a pitch that pierced my eardrums.*

*Minister Fumch approached and pressed a hypospray into my stomach.*

***

That was the last memory I had until the two Space Orcs rescued me from the caverns of Mars.

Not once, but for a second time in my life, I'd been duped by the promise of space exploration. But that was the last time. I wanted nothing more than to go back to my quiet life on Earth.

What was I thinking? I was too old to be chasing a dream that had almost faded away.

The image of my small bungalow a few blocks from the beach filled my mind. Just let me get back to Earth. Just let me get back to Earth. I said it over and over in my mind until the pain meds from the medical pod started to work, and darkness took over.

# CHAPTER 4: Chozek Dromi - Space Orc

I was furious. We all were. Each of us individually, and all of us collectively. Had those who brought her to Mars not already been dead, I would have killed each of them with my claws, weapons be damned.

She was beautiful, even in her broken form. I had held her close to me as we hastened from the bowels of that forsaken planet. Her heart had beat against mine. She was mine, ours.

I felt it. My brothers felt it. The battle rage within each of us was only held at bay by the urgency of removing her from danger.

My brothers and I spoke no words, each of us working seamlessly toward one goal, getting her to safety.

The comms pinged as my brothers made contact.

"We have a short window to bring you on board. I am sending the coordinates to you now," Shavrek said.

"She will be fine once we get her back to our ship, brother," Whorvek said, sensing my concern.

"They treated her in such a manner to draw us out. She would have died, and the fault would lie with us," I responded bitterly.

While we concerned ourselves with our ship's weaponry and our internal disputes, the fragile human female was being abused, battered, and left for dead.

I was angry at the Gernicians, the Avian, the Tekaari, and most certainly Orcqlaneasus.

Silently, we worked to meet our brothers at the appointed rendezvous point. Gernician ships surrounded us, and there was nothing I wanted more than to kill each of them for the pain they had inflicted on our precious passenger. The time was not now, however, since her welfare was paramount to all other concerns.

With stealth and ease, our shuttle docked within our ship. Whorvek secured the shuttle, and I once again carried our precious cargo, this time to our fully stocked medical bay.

Even though she had only spent a short time in the med pod, much of the inflammation around her eyes and face had lessened, making her even more beautiful to my eyes.

I knew that I was not worthy, but for a moment, I dared to imagine her in my arms, not as a helpless victim, but as a passionate mate. I rebuked my thoughts and turned my concern to seeing to her well-being only. I was ashamed that I had entertained such musings.

I was headed toward the medical bay with her when Whorvek caught up to me.

"Take her by the bridge. Our brothers should see that we have secured her safely, to ease their concerns as ours have been," he said.

I understood the request, and since she had improved, I agreed and took our fragile passenger to the ship's bridge while she continued to sleep peacefully in my arms.

Surprisingly, Ghorvik was the first to approach.

"You should not have brought her here. It is not yet safe. Take her to the medical bay immediately," he roared, contrary as always, before returning to his station.

"Ghorvik is right. I appreciate the gesture, but she should be in the medical bay. You might also want to have the Pstoadys examine her," Shavrek offered.

"The Pstoadys, I am not sure she needs them. Do they not pose a threat to her as well? I thought that was why they were detained in the first place, for the threat they posed to human females," Whorvek said, mirroring my thoughts exactly.

"Fine. But we are going to need all of us to get out of this Gernician snare with the limited firepower that we have. We will not be able to see to the human and navigate what must be done. She will likely be fine alone in the med bay. The sensors will alert us if there is a problem."

We all knew what Shavrek was doing, and we equally admired and resented him for it. He had a way of pointing out the things we did not want to see, often saying the things we did not want to hear.

Sensing the strife in the air, Whorvek stepped in, as he always did, to set our course of action.

Begrudgingly, he said, "Shavrek is correct. The Pstoadys are our best hope in helping her heal. That is why we brought them, so we might as well use their expertise."

I turned with her in my arms to take her to the med bay, not certain that bringing the Pstoadys was the best course of action, but seeing no other option.

"Brother, wait. I will have a word with the Pstoadys and then release them to attend our guest," Ghorvik said.

Smiling to myself, I knew how profound a word from Ghorvik could be. I felt much more assured that the two alien scientists would be inclined to help our human without any of their additional enhancements.

As I turned to leave the bridge, my human began to cough uncontrollably. She appeared unconscious still, but struggled to breathe as her body seized. I ran from the bridge, regretting my foolish decision to stop and reassure my brethren. It had been a selfish act, not placing her welfare above our own. I vowed to never make the same mistake again, if given the opportunity.

I reached the med bay, where Ghorvik and the Pstoadys were waiting. I settled my human onto the medical cot before placing her in the more advanced pod. The med pod on the shuttle had healed most of the surface damage to her beautiful face. Though still slightly bruised, it was no longer swollen or covered in blood and grime.

I knew from experience that the med pod worked best when the patient inside was unclothed.

I did not know, however, if I should be the one to remove her clothing. As it was, her shirt was shorn, and I found myself constantly averting my eyes from her extremely large breasts. They were so massive it would take both of my claws to gather just one.

Fuck. Again, my thoughts betrayed me.

Quickly, I stepped away from the helpless female beauty lying before me.

Momentarily, Ghorvik entered with the two identical Pstoady scientists, chatting back and forth, finishing each other's sentences in a manner that was truly confounding. Looking and listening to them was like hearing someone's inner dialogue spoken aloud. Ghorvik seemed flustered, whereas the Pstoadys were animated.

Seeing the patient on the medical cot, they immediately went to work, ignoring both Ghorvik and me.

"Greetings, Warrior Chozek. It is our honor to care for your human," the shorter Pstoady said.

"She is not our human, Tovak. Get her well so that she can return to her home," I said, exasperated by their assumption that she belonged to me.

"I am Torvak. My brother is Tovak," he responded.

"We will care for your human," the other one said.

The frustration I felt was reflected on Ghorvik's face.

"Brother, we must return to the bridge. We cannot protect her from here."

I would have lingered, but my brother's words were clarifying. I looked at the Pstoadys, who had already taken charge of their patient. They had her disrobed and on a hoverbed in a matter of seconds.

As I walked out of the med bay, they had secured her in the med pod, and one of them, I could not tell which, administered a hypospray to her sleeping form.

***

Back on the bridge, each of us took our stations. Although we dared not speak them aloud, the human in the medical bay was preeminent in our thoughts.

"Chozek, find us a way out of this shitstorm. Shavrek, be ready to punch us through as soon as he loads in the coordinates," Ghorvik barked from the captain's chair.

"I found some other surprises on this ship that will keep those see-through bastards at bay. We possess a sonic missile concealed in our comms array that will disorient the Gernicians and crack their crystalline ships when deployed. That should give us enough time to bring in the M.A.S.T. and get the hell out of here," he said.

"I see a way out. It is straight through the center of their fleet. Once Whorvek fires up the sonic missile, we have one shot for Shavrek to fly us out of here," I said, eager to put our plan into action.

We glanced at each other, each set in his role, waiting for Ghorvik to give the command.

"Execute."

Immediately, Whorvek deployed the sonic missile, and the outer hulls of each of the Gernician ships splintered apart.

"Now that, brothers, is a very pretty sight," Ghorvik laughed. "Shavrek, take us out of here."

Shavrek immediately engaged our newly fitted hyperdrive engines. Using them required that we drop our M.A.S.T., making us visible to our enemy, if only momentarily. It was a calculated risk, and I hoped these engines worked, but as they were yet untested, there was no way to know with certainty.

I had felt the jolt between Galactic Standard and hyperspeed hundreds of times as an intergalactic space warrior, but this was something different. None of us was prepared for the jump from stationary to hyperspeed with these engines.

There was a sudden change in air pressure, and gravity lifted each of us from our posts before slamming us back down onto the bridge's floor.

"What the fuck was that?" Whorvek grumbled.

"That was the Earth Mother's new hyperspeed invention. Shavrek, power down these fucking engines and take us back to Galactic Standard. Where did that leave us in the galaxy?"

Shavrek responded quickly, "I charted a path, once clear of the Gernicians, toward Earth's moon. If we are planning to return the human home, that is the best course before us."

I heard the uncontrollable growl that left my throat, however futile. Logic dictated that we return the human we had rescued back home, but I did not want to let her go.

"That was a sound decision. The Gernicians used her as bait to ensnare us. She deserves to return home safely. Perhaps we should check on her and the Pstoadys to see how they fared during our shift to hyperspeed," Whorvek reasoned.

"I will also attend, brother," I said, with a mix of anger, impatience, and agitation.

***

As we made our way through the ship toward the medical bay, we encountered a series of shipwide malfunctions.

Emergency lights sputtered and blinked. As we entered the darkened medical bay, an emergency klaxon peeled incessantly.

I looked around and did not see the Pstoadys. More importantly, I did not see my human.

"She is not here. What the fuck did they do with her?" I said.

"See if you can get some power in here. What the fuck happened?" Whorvek demanded.

I tried to use the shipwide intercom from the medical bay to alert the bridge to the chaos unfolding before us, but received no response.

"Internal comms are out, too. You need to go to the bridge and get our brothers so that we can conduct a shipwide search," I said over the blare of the klaxon.

As Whorvek turned to leave, I added, "See if you can do anything about this fucking noise!"

Whorvek headed toward the bridge, and I took off in the opposite direction in search of my human.

# CHAPTER 5: Angela's Moon Dance

I was rudely awakened from the warm healing pod I had been placed in by the two Space Orcs who had found me.

I'd been having the sexiest, most erotic dream I had ever had, featuring my green heroes, before I was jolted awake and urged out of my pod by two small Pstoady medical techs.

I'd seen vids of aliens like them before during updates from the Distant Wars. My university had also participated in a virtual exchange with their education ministry.

Their species valued intellectual curiosity, so seeing them in real life gave me some measure of assurance, considering my present situation.

The med pod opened, and there they were, introducing themselves to me.

"I am Torvak," one said.

"I am Tovak," said the other.

"We are here to help you heal," one said.

"But the ship is now under attack, and we must flee to safety," the other said.

I struggled to follow their quick words as they volleyed their discourse back and forth like a tennis match.

"You must leave the med pod and hide."

"We will help you."

"The Space Orcs will find you."

"They will help you."

"They will care for you."

"You will be safe."

"Yes, they will keep you safe."

"We must hurry."

"There is no time. We must leave now."

As I stood up from the med pod, I realized I wasn't wearing a stitch of clothing. Sensing my embarrassment, the Pstoadys turned their backs to me and pulled a sheet from a nearby medical cot.

I wrapped it around me, toga-style, and stood unsteadily.

"We have hyposprays for you."

"Yes, hyposprays will help you heal quickly."

"I've never used one of those before. I don't know how to," I said in utter confusion.

"We will teach you."

The taller of the Pstoadys moved my sheet dress aside to expose a patch of skin. He then pressed the hypospray against my skin and depressed the trigger to release the medication.

Instantly, I felt relief. This alien medication was truly a wonder. Just a short while ago, I had been so banged up that I could barely walk, and now I was up and about, preparing to take flight on my own accord.

I started to walk out of the room and felt a sharp pain in my hip, moaning in response.

"Use the hypospray."

"Yes, use the hypospray. It will heal you."

I pressed the hypospray, as the alien had shown me, directly over the pain radiating from my hip.

Again, the pain vanished instantly.

"Follow us."

"We will help you hide."

"Do not worry."

"The Space Orcs will come for you."

I followed the small aliens down the hallway with blinking lights, and I wondered about my future.

It was weird, though. I felt detached from everything around me. I was at peace and calm. It had to be the work of the alien tranquilizer I'd jabbed myself with, but if it kept me feeling this good, I didn't care. Still, I asked the hard questions.

"Um, how much of this can I take?" I asked. "This won't turn me into some kind of alien junkie, dependent on whatever's in this hypospray just to make it day by day?"

"No, you can take as much as you need to heal."

"You will not become addicted to it."

"It will help you."

"Do not worry."

"The Space Orcs will come for you."

"All will be well," they said in eerie unison.

Just as I was getting tired from following the Pstoadys throughout the ship, they led me to a large stateroom.

"Hide in here," they said together.

"Get some rest."

"The Space Orcs will come for you."

"I don't know. I'm too anxious to sleep. Do you really think the other aliens will board the ship?"

"The Space Orcs will come for you."

"Use the hypospray."

"You need your rest."

Following their advice, I climbed into the large bed in the stateroom. I was so tired, it was hard to keep my eyes open.

I saw the Pstoadys creeping from the room. "Where are you going?" They didn't respond at first.

"You need your rest."

"The Space Orcs will find you."

That's the last thing I heard as my subconscious took over and I dreamed once more of green flesh on brown flesh.

The dream was so vivid it was hard to know when it ended, especially when I heard the raspy voice of one of the Space Orcs from before, though I wasn't sure which one.

"Wake up, human. I am here."

It was Whorvek, or maybe Chozek, but for some reason he called me "human" instead of my name, which was weird considering it was my dream. That was my first cue that I wasn't dreaming anymore.

Sleepily, I replied, "I am not human, I'm Angela, Angela Thomas." Yawning, I corrected myself. "I mean, I am human, but my name is Angela. Dr. Angela Thomas."

"Angela, a beautiful name for a beautiful human," he said, smiling at me.

That smile did something to me, coming off my hot-ass dream. My pussy gushed. Damn, that was embarrassing. What if his alien senses picked up on the sound, or worse yet, the scent? I mean, I'd been buried alive and grimy and stank, but I seemed clean now. Oh yeah, the med pod must have sanitized me, freaky alien technology. Fuck, I was spiraling again, but that was better than thinking about jumping all over his sexy ass, whatever his name was.

"Considering your earlier state, you have made a remarkable recovery."

I tried to respond normally. "The Pstoadys helped me with their magical hyposprays."

In a flash, his expression changed. He flexed his claws, and my eyes clocked every movement.

"Fucking Pstoadys, they did exactly what we instructed them not to do," he grumbled.

His sexy voice dropped an octave with his anger. Every word he spoke made me hotter and hotter. I squeezed my legs together, squirming on the bed, my pussy pulsing to the vibrato of his voice.

"Stop, please, don't say another word," I panted.

My eyes drank him in, a beautiful, sculpted jade marvel at the foot of my bed. Damn, green was my new favorite color.

Fuck it. I pulled the sheet from my body and exposed myself to him. "Something's wrong. I'm hot, right here," I said, stroking my pussy in front of him.

He placed his clawed hand on my thigh, and I opened my legs wide so he could see how wet I was.

He growled, and I lay back, spreading my legs wider, an unspoken invitation, because I was too needy to form another word.

"Angela, I am an Orcqlaneasion, and as much as I want to fuck you and make you mine, I think you need to know what is going on."

He seemed conflicted. Even though he was an alien, he was still male, and I could see by the huge dick print protruding from his tight leather pants that this wet ass pussy was affecting him.

He pulled me up into a sitting position and wrapped the sheet back around me.

"What is happening to you is beyond your control. The Pstoadys have infected you with a pheromone that makes your kind want to have sex and mate with my kind."

"I don't understand. Are you saying I want you because of the Pstoadys?"

"Yes, what you are feeling is caused by our pheromones."

Pheromones, no fucking way. He was trying to be noble or some shit, and all I wanted to do was fuck.

"No, that story doesn't hold water, because I thought you and your brother were hot even when you dug me out of my burial pit back on Mars."

He laughed, a rich, deep sound, and I felt the beginnings of an orgasm. I grabbed his dick in my hands.

"Pheromones or not, I'm a full-grown woman. A lot of shady shit has gone down, and I can't figure any of it out right now. Right now, I want to fuck," I said, massaging his leather-covered telephone pole length in my palms.

He pulled my hands away. "Orcqlaneasions do not just fuck. We mate for life. If you give yourself to me, you would also be giving yourself to my brothers in a lifetime bond."

Lifetime? Was he serious? I almost died twice, so life didn't seem so damn certain. Hell, it never had.

"Okay," I said. I just wanted to fuck this beautiful creature. I wanted to feel, to live. If I had to fuck his brothers into perpetuity, I would do whatever it took to get that alien dick inside me right now. I'd worry about the repercussions tomorrow.

I was tired of living a careful life. What had it ever gotten me besides stays in the psych ward, depression, and regret for days and weeks on end. Whenever I stepped off the predetermined path, everything went to shit. I couldn't think about that now. My brain was too fuzzy.

I focused my attention on Whorvek, Chozek, whoever the fuck this was.

I watched his face to see what his decision would be. He took off his scabbard that held the weapons across his chest, and I knew that he was mine.

I moaned as I lay back down on the bed, and this time, instead of wrapping me in the sheet, he tore it from my body and lifted my legs over his shoulders.

I felt his breath as he nudged his face between my thighs. I clenched my pussy to hold back the tsunami flood that I was about to release.

He put his claws on my big-ass apron belly, and normally a move like that would have embarrassed the fuck out of me, but the way he kneaded it with his claws was almost reverent.

I felt the tip of his tongue swipe my labia, and I fucking came, releasing the surge I'd been holding back. He drank my liquid heat like it filled a deep, empty thirst that could not be quenched. It was an erotic combination of sucking my pussy lips and pressing his tongue deep inside me, all while massaging my belly. I didn't know what that was about, maybe it was an erogenous zone, but I fucking came again as he made a gourmet feast out of my pussy.

I grabbed ahold of his dreads and held on as he gave me the most sensual oral attention I had ever experienced. Nobody had ever eaten me out like this before, even during my same-sex experimentation phase.

I was wrung out and tried to lift up, but he pushed me back down, pulled his tongue out of my pussy, and then started licking me from my clit to my asshole, something no one of any sex had ever done to me before. Damn, this Space Orc was nasty as fuck, and I liked it.

He started fucking me again with his tongue. I was screaming my release, grabbing the sheets, looking for something to hold onto, when

Chozek, or was it Whorvek, walked into the cabin, finding me riding his brother's face.

He didn't look angry or upset, so I guess that whole "being with all of them" thing must be true. Fuck, I still didn't know which one was which, Chozek or Whorvek.

I would soon find out, since I beckoned him over with my finger.

He approached me rapidly, freeing himself of his weapons and pants. I laughed at how fast he stripped, and was rewarded with a hard suck to my clit that ramped up my moaning and panting even more.

Honing in on my large breasts, he gathered one in both of his claws and sucked on my nipple. The slight scrape of his fang against my areola had me coming again, and I begged the brothers for a moment to catch my breath.

Each complied. The one between my thighs said, "Somehow, I knew you would be the one to find us, brother."

The other one, still caressing my breast, said, "Not a moment too soon, by my estimation. Have you asked her to become our mate yet?"

Okay, so yes, I didn't know their names, and that was pretty bad, but they were pissing me off, talking about me like I wasn't there. I pushed my palm against titty-Orc's big green head to get his attention.

"I'm right fucking here. You don't get to talk about me like I'm not," I said angrily.

"Apologies, I did not mean it like that. I only meant to ask if he had asked for your consent. Fuck, this is not the way I expected this at all," he said in confusion.

"So, you expected me to want to fuck you and your brothers. That means you knew what the Pstoadys were planning to do to me."

"No, none of us knew, although the Pstoadys being who they are, it was always a calculated risk," he said.

"It seems like more of a risk to me and an opportunity for you," I said, coming down from my orgasm-induced high.

The other one, pussy-licker, although that name didn't do justice to what that Space Orc had me feeling, like dayum. Anyway, that one finally spoke, and in my head I kept hearing, "kitty cat got your tongue."

"It is your choice, as I explained to you, Angela, to decide to become our mate, but once you do, we become one."

"Angela, a beautiful name for a beautiful human," titty-orc said, repeating the same thing his brother had said earlier upon learning my name.

I sat there between them, confused as fuck, and not only about their names. I was open, exposed, questioning my sanity in even considering the proposal before me. Deep down, I didn't believe either of them. I knew their reputation as peacekeepers with a seemingly honorable moral compass, but I knew all too well from experience that a reputation didn't mean shit.

I couldn't go down memory lane now, though. Thinking about the past made my head hurt. My body was still fucked up, heavy, horny, and aching for dick. Fuck it, I would do it. So, what if they wanted to run an alien train on me? I was down. But even an old hoe like me wanted to know the name of the dick inside me. Shit, how many of them were there again? I think four, hopefully not more than that.

But what's the saying again? In for a penny, in for a pound-ing.

I smiled and made my decision.

# CHAPTER 6: Ghorvik Rhadi - Space Orc

This fucking ship made no fucking sense. Bouncing us across the galaxy faster than galactic standard, approaching hyperspeed, but with engines not quite powerful enough to reach it. Never battle-tested, not even flown from one quadrant to the next, and this is what we depended on for this fucking mission.

A mission that would not have been necessary in the first place if it had not been for the fucking human females. Like every other Orcqlaneasion male, I was grateful to them. How could I not be? They were bringing my race, my people, back from the brink of extinction, but they had upended our entire way of life in the process.

Never in all my annums had we rushed headlong into danger, heedless of the consequences, with only a vague hope of success. It was all directed by the alien Earth Mothers in the guise of the Directorate.

Our Directorate was hopelessly compromised, led by Chief Elder Illbrien Rezz, who had always been on the precipice of sanity. Then we find he has hidden an unmoored brother for two decades, and if that is not heinous enough, he goes and copulates with a human, solidifying his lineage and tightening his grip on the hierarchy.

My brothers and I were less than one annum away from becoming elders. Our last mission was to secure the area around the planet Mars. But before we could install our security grid, we received a distress call from our brethren, elders entrusted with a human mate and those fucking Pstoady scientists.

Those little fuckers have been the bane of my existence. Bringing them on this mission was another example of an insane command from the Directorate, especially knowing how much havoc they could wreak.

True to form, they sabotaged this fucking ship moments after we retreated from our scuffle with the Gernicians, forcing us to land on Earth's moon. It was the last place I wanted to be, but it would give us a chance to offload our human cargo and see her back to Earth. That is, of course, if I could keep my brothers from sticking their cocks in her.

I felt their lust through our bond connection, and I was not alone. Shavrek followed close on my heels as we tore through the ship, rushing to the stateroom to prevent our brothers from bonding us to this unknown human female.

More determined than I to abort this impending bonding, Shavrek tore past me, reaching the stateroom before I did, where our brothers and the human waited. I stopped short at the scene in front of me.

Whorvek was sitting on the bed with his cock wedged down the human's throat as she struggled to take him in, while Chozek was behind her, feasting on her pussy. His claws were imprinted on her large brown ass.

I was speechless at the sight, but Shavrek was not.

"Brothers, cease. We are not in accord in this mating. Leave the human now," he growled.

In response, both Whorvek and Chozek returned his answering growl while the human pulled a release from Whorvek's cock. Cum spilled from her lips as she used her tongue to lick him clean. She stopped, and we witnessed her body tense before she screamed through her own climax that Chozek had initiated between her thighs.

She crawled up next to Whorvek, who wrapped his arms around her in a show of protection that left no room for misinterpretation. Chozek took position on her other side, equally defiant, providing an unmistakable shield for the human he had just brought to completion.

"Dr. Angela Thomas has agreed to be our mate. There is no question that this will happen," Chozek said.

"We have not discussed taking a mate, brothers. Such a thing was never even possible before, so it was never an issue. But a decision of such magnitude should only be taken in consultation with all of us," Shavrek said.

Finally finding my voice, I lent my support.

"Our mission, brothers, was to rescue the human and return her to Earth. We are currently on Earth's moon. We should place her on a transport and return her to her people unscathed," I said with full authority in my role as captain.

"Unscathed?" Angela screamed. "I was left to die on an isolated planet, thrown into an underground ravine, buried alive, then 'rescued' and conveniently pumped full of sex pheromones so y'all could run a train on me. And hell, I was kinda down with it, because y'all fine as fuck, but how the fuck is that unscathed?"

I was confused by the human's language. She used words in an unfamiliar manner that my universal translator could not decode in the correct context. What would human mass transportation have to do with our mating ritual?

Whorvek pulled the human closer to him, clearly as confused as the rest of us.

"Angela, explain the train reference. We have adjusted our translators to include many of your African-American Vernacular English phrases, but this one escapes us."

She laughed heartily, disengaging herself from my brothers, and wrapped the sheet tightly around her body.

"Okay, this is actually my thing, or my area of study, I should say. I'm gonna stop code-switching on y'all and step into my vocation as an alien cultural anthropologist, Dr. Angela M. Thomas," she said, smiling.

"I know this is awkward, but give me a little grace, okay? I've been through a helluva lot," she continued.

Chozek moved closer to her and took her hand in his claw.

"I am glad that we found you before further irreparable damage could be wrought. But you have my sincere apologies for your misadventure," he said.

She pulled her hand away and clutched his face in her hands.

"It's not your fault, and I am sincerely grateful that you saved me." Turning to look from Chozek to Whorvek and then to Shavrek and me, she continued, "All of you saved me, and I am sincerely grateful."

"Running a train is a slang term for when one man has sex with a woman, followed by another, and then another, one after the other," she explained.

Understanding this context, my brethren and I were equally shocked and offended that the human would think so little of us. We were honorable Orcqlaneasion males, still in our prime, moving toward the exalted state of elder. We would never debase or use a female in such a manner.

Each of my brothers gave in to a low growl to express their disdain at the mischaracterization.

"Why are y'all growling? What's going on?" she asked worriedly.

Although I had mixed feelings about the human, and I in no way wanted a lifetime commitment with her, I nevertheless did not want her to fear us.

I took a step toward her, and she retreated into Whorvek's waiting arms, which unconsciously caused me to growl again.

"Angela, we do not wish to harm you. Our growls can indicate our anger, but we are not angry at you. We are angered that you would think we would use you in such a manner," I said.

She looked at all of us, confused. "I don't understand. I thought that you wanted to have sex with me, all of you." Pulling away from Whorvek and wrapping the sheet tighter around her body, she moved off the bed. "I'm so embarrassed. I mean, of course you don't want to have sex with me. You're like the superheroes of the galaxy, and I'm a fat, neurotic, middle-aged xenoanthropologist."

She walked past Shavrek and me toward the small cabinet in the stateroom. Helplessly, Shavrek and I stared at each other while Chozek and Whorvek amplified their growls, this time directed at us. We had intended to put a stop to the mating process with the human, but we had not meant to cause her further pain by rejecting her.

Garnering our attention again, we watched as the human pressed a tainted hypospray into her rounded belly.

"No, you must not," Shavrek said, grabbing her hand and crushing the hypospray with his claw, but it was too late. Angela had given herself yet another dose of the pheromone that made her body compatible with ours and put her in human "heat." At least that was how it was described to us by the Earth Mothers.

"What the fuck! I feel like shit. I'm hot, horny, basically falling apart, and you take the only relief that I have. Fuck y'all Space Orcs. Get the fuck out and leave me alone."

I could feel the human's anger, so I tried to speak calmly in an effort to reassure her that we would never hurt her, intentionally or not.

"Angela, the pheromone was in the hypospray the Pstoadys gave you. Your body is in heat, and there is no remedy or antidote for it other than copulation."

"Are you saying I just gave myself another dose of the sex pheromone? How long does it take to wear off?" she asked miserably.

I looked at the human, the need to protect her at odds with the words I must speak that would cause her further pain.

"The pheromone does not wear off. Instead, the symptoms intensify, and without relief, you will perish."

"Perish, as in die? You have to be fucking kidding me. Of course, sex is the only relief. How very fucking convenient," she said.

She stared at each of us as she seemed to process the information.

"I don't understand. You just told me you don't want to have sex with me, so what's the point of all this rescue shit if I still end up dying on top of being horny as fuck?"

Seeing her distress, Chozek rushed to her side and gathered her in his arms.

"We want far more than sex with you. We wish to mate with you, protect you, share our lifebound with you. We want to give you our seed and create the next generation of Orcqlaneasion warriors."

She looked up at his gaze through teary eyes. "That's a lot. I don't know if I want to be a whole mate. Can we just have sex and you go your way and I go mine? I mean, how would that work? I have a life on Earth, a career, a home. I can't see y'all living on Earth, and I don't want to go to your homeworld. I've worked too hard for the life I've created for myself."

Chozek leaned down and kissed away her tears. "Let us care for you, my Anjua. Agree to become our mate, and we will create a future together, however that looks."

In a quiet voice, she hugged him and whispered, "They don't want me."

My blood boiled, impotent fury with no release for the pain I had caused my mate. I could not, I would not, let her bear the sting of my rejection another second.

I reached for her and pulled her from Chozek's arms, surprising them both. Fear filled her eyes as I lifted her and placed her on the empty bed. I heard Chozek growl behind me, but from my periphery, I saw Shavrek holding him back.

I gently unwrapped the sheet covering her lush body. Still, she looked at me with uncertainty, her brown eyes hesitant, her tear-streaked cheeks evidence of my earlier rejection etched on her skin. I leaned in and licked her tears away, tasting her salty warmth and her reticence at this sudden turn.

This would take us from our predetermined path. Elders of the Directorate, each of us whole and committed to Orcqlaneasus. In time, I had hoped to become Chief Elder and restore order and sanity to our world. But seeing this fragile being entrusted to me by Laneasus herself, all my plans and ambitions shifted. I knew with certainty that this was my destiny.

She was my destiny.

I kissed her cheeks again and moved downward, kissing her smooth neck, her bountiful breasts, her rounded belly, and the apex of her thighs.

I stood, released my cock from the confines of my leather leggings, and placed it at the mouth of her pussy.

Heat rolled off her in waves as her body emanated the human perspiration her kind was known for.

"Dr. Angela Thomas of Earth, will you take my seed, bear my young, be my chosen mate, and share my life bond with my brethren?"

There was a moment of hesitation, but she responded, "Yes," and I pressed my thick cock inside her.

She was tight, and I recognized that I might hurt her, but the Pstoady pheromones not only encouraged human estrus, they also made their bodies pliable to the size of our cocks without pain or discomfort.

I drove into her without restraint, the way she clenched around me and her moans of rapture making it clear she could take it.

She would have to. She was not only my mate, but the mate to three other Orcqlaneasion warriors still in their prime, each eager to wet their cock in their chosen mate and create the next generation.

As if invading my thoughts, Shavrek appeared beside my Anjua. He shared my reluctance to mate with the human, for reasons his own. He leaned down and kissed her, his claws wrapping in the tight coils of her black, gray, and white hair.

She responded by squeezing my cock deep within her womb, and I almost spent my cum in answer. But forcefully, I regained her attention by pushing one of her legs up and pressing deeper inside her.

Shavrek, sensing a challenge in gaining our mate's attention, rose and presented his cock to her lips. For all the lushness of her body, her small human mouth could not take in his warrior's girth. She licked and sucked, but amazingly, Shavrek continued pressing his cock down into her throat.

She was a warrior's mate, and we took her as such, giving her no rest. Her body tightened over and over, one climax following another. I met her final release with my own as my cum flooded her womb, seeding her with future progeny. Shavrek followed, and just as she had captured Whorvek's cum earlier, she eagerly drank down Shavrek's.

Reluctantly, I pulled from her body, feeling my brother's presence nearby. She held onto me as if she did not want to let me go.

Shavrek pulled her arms away, and I left her grasp, at least momentarily. I would give my brethren their time with her, but her body was made to accommodate ours without limit, and I planned to test that theory on my new mate.

Shavrek lay on the bed and pulled our mate across his lap. He sat up, embraced her, and began the consent ritual required of all Orcqlaneasion males.

"Alluring human Dr. Angela Thomas, I am called Shavrek Trangi, and I would take you as my mate and claim you, just as my brother Ghorvik Rhadi has already done," he said with humor.

Of course, Shavrek would realize that I mated with Angela without giving her my name. Although it was technically not required, it was awkward that she had agreed to become my mate without knowing it. I was equal parts thankful and annoyed with Shavrek for covering my error.

He continued with the familiar words. "Angela will become my mate, bear my sons, and share my bond and life force."

In answer, my mate, our mate, said, "I will."

Shavrek lifted her up and placed her on his ready cock. We all heard the squelch of her soaked pussy as Shavrek filled her. He leaned back, lying on the bed.

"Ride your mate, human. Ride your warrior," he said arrogantly.

Impatient as I was to be with my mate again, I quashed the urge to pull her from Shavrek and retreated into a corner to watch him pleasure our mate, or perhaps her pleasure him with reckless abandon.

But I was not the only brother impatient for our mate. Both Chozek and Whorvek approached together, moving in on either side of her as she bobbed up and down on Shavrek's cock. My brothers each took one of her large brown breasts in their claws. Whorvek kneaded and pinched the one in his grasp, whereas Chozek sucked the other into his mouth, nursing frantically like the babe she would one day carry.

In my mind, I kept imagining that my son was already growing deep within her, from where I had planted him a few moments earlier.

My, our mate climaxed, most probably from the attention of my brethren Chozek and Whorvek, which seemed to peeve Shavrek. He waved his claw, indicating that he wanted our brothers to move away. Begrudgingly, each one did.

Shavrek lifted Angela off his cock and placed her on her arms and elbows across the bed, her ass hanging off the edge. He stepped behind her and ruthlessly pushed his cock back inside her pussy while pressing her head down into the bed.

I felt a growl rise in my throat at his callous treatment of her, but I tried to contain it. Surprisingly, Angela screamed, "Yes, yes!" over and over again, a clear indication that she was in no distress from Shavrek's brutal fucking.

Shavrek pummeled our mate, pressing his claws into her shoulders, rendering her immobile. With each thrust into her, I felt my ire rise. Not because he was fucking her. She was his mate as much as she was mine. But the savage treatment left me shaken. Whatever his issues were with her, he had still not resolved them, and the way he mated her made that point lethally sharp.

When he finally released his seed inside her, I let out a breath I did not realize I had been holding. He pulled out of her, his seed dripping from his cock and her pussy, turned, picked up his clothes, and left the stateroom.

I left my place in the darkened corner of the room where I had been witness to my brother's mating with Angela to lend her comfort. But before I could, Chozek had already lifted her over his shoulder and bounced her onto the bed.

I growled at his treatment of her when she laughed, a rich and hearty sound filled with the passion of the previous endeavors. Chozek and Whorvek bounded next to her on either side, equally sharing in her mirth before their sounds of merriment soon gave rise to cries of passion.

Each of my brothers, working in tandem, lavished her body with attention, stroking and sucking her neck and breasts while moving lower, caressing her belly, tonguing her navel, scoring her skin with their claws. And our mate basked in the attention.

Whorvek pushed her onto her side and slid behind her. He lifted one of her legs, and moisture seeped in rivulets from her weeping pussy, full from Shavrek, myself, and her own passions.

From his position behind her, he continued the mating ritual by uttering the words that would bind her to us even more.

"Angela, do you consent to becoming my mate, sharing my life, my bond, and bearing my sons?"

Before she could respond, Chozek moved in front of her so that she was caught between my brothers, one on either side of her. He too spoke the mating words to her.

"Angela, will you also become my mate and complete our life bond, share my heart, my body, and my life force, and nurture the sons I plant in your body?"

Again, she gave a small laugh before giving her response to both brothers.

"Okay, this is a lot, but yes to you, Whorvek, and to you, Chozek. I consent to being your mate."

"Anjua, you are mistaken. I am Chozek, and he is Whorvek. Have you not known which one of us has pleasured you?" Chozek asked.

"I, um, no, I'm sorry," she said.

Hearing her response, Chozek lifted her leg over his thigh, and Whorvek thrust into her from behind. He pulled out, and then Chozek pushed inside her from the front. This continued as each brother see-sawed in and out of her pussy at a relentless pace, fucking her in tandem, a primal breeding of the human we now all called our mate.

I was overcome by the sounds of her passion as she screamed her release, climax after climax consuming her body. I could hold back no more, wedging myself between her and Chozek, presenting her pretty lips with my cock.

As she screamed her release, my brother Chozek growled and lodged his seed within her. He retreated from her body and mushed me in the back of my head for encroaching on his space with our mate.

Undaunted, I continued feeding her my cock as she greedily took in more and more. Lodged deep in the tight confines of her throat, I was completely undone when she screamed once more, cumming together with Whorvek.

As he emptied his seed in her womb, I spilled mine down her welcoming throat. It was the culmination of a mating I had never imagined, never dreamed was possible.

Chozek returned to his place next to our mate on the bed, indicating with a nod that I could stay, but my position would be next to her feet at the bottom of the massive bed, while Whorvek remained behind her.

From my position, I played with her small human toes. She gave a tired laugh, exhausted, no doubt, from being mated and bred. Content in my new role as mate to a human, I gave in to lethargy and slept, secure in the knowledge that my future was certain, and my brothers and I were no longer in jeopardy of being the last of our kind.

# CHAPTER 7: Angela's Escape

I've had sex before, and no small amount of it. Back in the day, I would fuck a nigga and be done with the quickness. For all my degrees and education, I've found it to be a great stress reliever to come on an anonymous dick before a big test or some other momentous event. Back then, I would frequent any little hole-in-the-wall club down on Sistrunk and get my freak on. But as soon as I got a hoe reputation, I'd have to find another one. Yeah, the brothers could fuck the taste out of my mouth, but even that didn't compare with my time with my new alien mates.

It was quite literally a fucking frenzy. And for all that, I felt better than I've ever felt in my life. Like I could climb a mountain, slay a dragon, or just fuck a motherfucker up. I don't know when I've ever had this much energy before. I wasn't even sore, which in itself was mind-blowing considering the tree-trunk size of the Space Orcs' dicks. Whatever magic potion those little toad-like aliens had cooked up must have made me elastic inside. Because just from an anatomical perspective, they had to have breached my cervix, and just thinking about that shit is painful. But here I stand, "unscathed," to quote my alien lovers. And that's how I thought of them.

They were my alien lovers, and that was it. Yeah, I consented to be with them as their mate, but as soon as I returned to Earth, I would get whatever the equivalent of an alien divorce was, assuming, of course, I was even aligned to them in some sort of binding way.

It's funny that each of them talked about me having babies, but what they didn't know was that I was well past menopause. On top of that, I only had one good ovary after my "incident" several years ago. I didn't want to think about that now. I was feeling too good. Plus, I had to plot my escape from my alien rescuers.

The first step, though, was untangling myself from the bed. I was literally surrounded by rugged, muscle-bound masculinity in different shades of green. Shit, no matter what happened, green would always be my favorite color, and drinking mint tea would never be the same again. I mean, their jizz was mint-flavored, the fuck. That alone was addicting as hell. It was like they were created by the Goddess to be perfect in every way. That didn't matter, though, because I had a life to get back to.

Fuck, there was absolutely no way to move without waking one of them while trying to leave.

While I was contemplating my escape, I heard a raspy voice from the foot of the bed. "Angela, my mate, I hear that you are awake. Do you need to relieve yourself in the lavatory?"

I think his name was Ghorvik. He seemed to be the most seasoned of the group, with battle scars on his face and crisscrossing his chest.

"Yeah, I do need to go pretty badly. I was trying to figure out how to disentangle myself," I said lightly. And just like that, my lover to the left and my lover to the right moved their arms that had been cuddling me, and all of them bounded from the bed faster than humanly possible, reminding me yet again, *Sis, you fucked some aliens!*

Still in amazement at their lightning speed, Chozek picked me up and started walking toward what I assumed to be the lavatory.

"Um, I can walk to the bathroom, err, lavatory, on my own," I said, laughing.

"It gives me pleasure to carry my mate, but I will release you if it bothers you," he said, with what seemed like a pout, but maybe that was me imagining that.

"Chozek, release our mate. Humans require privacy for their bodily functions," Whorvek said in admonishment.

"It's okay," I said to Chozek to reassure him, although why I wasn't sure. He put me down, and I walked away from my three fierce alien warriors for my first moment of solitude since I'd awoken on this ship.

The lavatory was surprisingly human-looking, with a few exceptions. This was really my first time examining alien architecture, and my natural curiosity won out. I noticed all the small differences between Space Orc technology and human technology that spoke to their culture.

For instance, the lavatory didn't have mirrors. It wasn't a big thing, but learning about alien cultures was my entire field of study, and even this lavatory held a treasure trove of information.

I made quick use of the toilet because, again, I was fascinated by the subtle differences between their culture and human culture.

The shower unit looked amazing, but it was also another alien marvel. I was standing inside it, trying to figure out how to use it, when Whorvek entered unannounced.

"I am sorry for entering without your permission, but I thought to answer any questions you may have about how to use the facilities."

I turned and smiled at him, and he stepped inside the unit with me. He moved his clawed hand over an invisible panel that lit up, and he showed me how to turn on the water, soap, and dryer feature. It was almost like a car wash, but for people or aliens. I tried to pay attention, but the proximity to him was heating me up all over again. It wasn't as intense as it had been yesterday, but being this close to him had my body tingling all over.

"Would you like me to stay and assist you?" he asked, tempting me beyond all measure.

All my ladybits were screaming don't let him leave, but my brain took control and I knew if I got started with him, getting back to Earth would be the furthest thing to my mind.

"I'm good, but I need clothes. You don't happen to have a female human wardrobe stashed on this ship, no questions asked," I joked, trying to lighten the mood.

"We have nothing hidden on our ship, but we are docked on your planet's moon, so there are several purveyors of human goods and clothing available here. Let us know what you need, and we will secure it and have it to you once you leave the cleansing unit."

Immediately, my spidey senses kicked in. "Did you say we're on the moon? When did we get here? I can finally go home." I said the last part out loud, unwittingly disclosing my desire to return to Earth.

The atmosphere immediately changed between us. Whorvek started walking toward the lav door.

"We will secure attire for you, and then you can discuss your intentions with all of your mates."

He left, and I said out loud to myself, "This is going to be a problem."

***

Entering the stateroom after my space-age shower, I found the clothes the Space Orcs had left for me. There was a sexy, strappy, flowing, muumuu-type dress and a pair of clog-like sandals. Of course, they hadn't thought of underwear, and I wondered if that was an alien thing, a male thing, or some combination of both.

I threw on the dress and twirled around. I wish I had a mirror to check myself out, but I knew that between my big ass boobs and fat ass, I was poppin' this dress.

Just I began to wonder how I would find my alien lovers, there was a chime at the sliding panel door, and it opened as Chozek entered. It was a toss-up to me between him and Whorvek as to which one was the most fine. Chozek seemed like he was probably the youngest, although they were all at least my age, marked by the white streaking their black strands.

"You are beautiful," he said approaching me with a smile, and I caught a glimpse of what appeared to be a fang. Rather than being freaked out, I thought it was sexy as hell.

My ass was too old to be blushing, but I felt giddy as fuck, and I knew I probably had a goofy ass grin spread across my face.

He stepped right into my space, green as fresh-cut grass, with smooth eight-pack abs and that dangerous smile. All I wanted to do was taste him, and taking in the visible bulge in his pants, he wouldn't have minded at all.

"I am supposed to bring you to our, what is your human word for it, mess hall, so that you get some nourishment and discuss your plan to return to Earth with us," he said.

Damn, I completely forgot about everything with this Space Orc hovering over me. The sooner I got away from them, the better. I mumbled an unintelligible, "I'm ready," and followed him to the mess hall.

They were all there waiting on me. Even Mr. Hit-it-and-quit-it, as I'd named Shavrek in my head, since he didn't stick around after getting his dick wet like the others.

I sat at the oval-shaped table, surrounded again by the Space Orcs, and Whorvek handed me a metal plate of what looked to be human food. I was too hungry to question it and immediately began eating. I noticed that they weren't.

"Y'all not eating?" I asked between bites.

Chozek responded, "We already have. We were just waiting on you."

Shavrek then spoke loudly, surprising me and causing me to choke on my alien breakfast.

"So, you wish to return to Earth. Do you expect your mates to live with you there?" he asked.

"I didn't expect to have mates when I returned to Earth, so I don't know how to answer that question," I quipped in reply.

"You do have mates. Four of them. My question stands. Do you expect your mates to live with you on Earth?"

Okay, Mr. Hostility wrapped in a pretty green package.

"We should go to Earth. There was a semblance of a plan being created prior to the arrival of the Earth Mothers on the planet to discuss the viability of an exchange program of sorts, allowing Orcqlaneasions to meet with potential mates. Since human females have proven to be optimal mates, perhaps this is an opportunity to embark upon negotiations for such an endeavor," Ghorvik said, surprising everyone assembled.

"This is the first that I have heard of any such plan. How did we not know of this?" Shavrek asked angrily.

"As the eldest of our brotherhood, in preparation for joining the Elder Directorate, I have already met with many of our Elder brethren and been privy to most matters of the Directorate," he said.

Whorvek, sensing my confusion at the turn of the conversation, sought to clarify.

"Angela, we are Orcqlaneasion warriors in our prime, but as you can see by the shades of gray and white in our locs, we are older. As our hair becomes white and our wisdom grows, we take our places in the Orcqlaneasion Directorate, creating the governing rules for our society, maintaining diplomatic relations with other alien civilizations, and vetting and assigning peacekeeping missions throughout the galaxy. Ghorvik has apparently embraced this new role as Elder, while the rest of us have not," he said solemnly.

I completely understood what he was saying. They were aging out of being warriors based on their society's cultural standards, being pushed into a different role, and not all of them were happy about it. There was so much here to mine as a cultural anthropologist, and I really wanted to dig in, but I wanted to go home more.

Maybe I could learn about their culture even more once they had left me on Earth and help them as a sort of liaison in their mission to build a pathway for human females to meet and acquire Space Orc mates.

In any event, there was a lot to unpack here, especially, it seemed, amongst themselves. My involvement was probably making everything worse, so the best thing to do would be to take myself off the chessboard and get back to my life.

"I'm not really sure of the process for aliens to go to Earth. Generally speaking, I don't think you can unless it's in a diplomatic mission of some sort. The World Court has strict rules about alien interaction with human society," I said, hoping to thwart their decision to follow me to Earth.

Chozek said brightly, "Then we shall become diplomats. We will take our place in the Directorate and act as ambassadors from our world to yours."

I gave a deep sigh. That totally was not what I was going for, but maybe if I agreed with this plan, I could get from under their collective thumbs, so to speak.

"That could work. You should go back to your planet and do whatever you need to do on your part to make that happen. Meanwhile, I will go back to Earth and start the ball rolling," I said, hoping to sound sincere.

"You want us to leave you alone on Earth?" Chozek questioned, as though the idea was completely foreign to him. For whatever reason, old boy was really into me, and I could not see him just taking off. On the one hand, it was sweet and adorable, but on the other hand, it was just too much and smothering.

"She is right. We should let her return to Earth, and we will contact the Directorate and alert them of our change in status. Even I admit that this could bode well for Orcqlaneasus," Shavrek said, much to the amazement of all of us.

Taking advantage of this new turn of events, I quickly stood from the table and started to leave.

"I would like to get a transport back to Earth as soon as possible. If we are in the central hub, I can figure it out in no time," I said, thinking that if everything worked out, I'd be in my backyard gazebo by early evening, reflecting on my mishaps in outer space.

"That will not be necessary. Chozek and Whorvek can escort you to a private shuttle and arrange conveyance. Ghorvik and I will prepare the ship for departure once you are safely on your way and they have returned," Shavrek stated matter-of-factly.

I was surprised at how smoothly everything was going. I mean, before they swore they were my lifemates, and now, just like that, they were sending me on my way. I mean, I didn't really want them around, I was just here for the sex, but damn, they could've pretended like the shit they said earlier mattered.

Fuck them. I was not about to feel any type of way over some alien dick, even if it was good as fuck.

"Well, okay, then. I guess I will hear from you when you get back from your homeworld."

I turned and walked away. I was excited to be going back to my old life, but somewhere deep inside me, I was really sad. It almost felt like grief for the chance of a life I was walking away from. But again, they didn't seem to be putting up much of a fight, so this was for the best.

# CHAPTER 8: Shavrek Trangi - Space Orc

Angela had barely left the ship with Chozek and Whorvek before Ghorvik exploded.

"What the fuck was that, Shavrek? Have you lost your mind? Do you really expect us to leave our mate behind on Earth?"

"Absolutely not, but it was apparent she was eager to return, and I want to know why. I want to know who this female is you were so ready to mate without any regard for who she is or her past," I explained.

"Her past does not matter, only her future does with us. How can we have a future with her if she thinks we are abandoning her and going back to Orcqlaneasus?"

"We are not abandoning her. Chozek and Whorvek have enough common sense to remember our warrior training and enact a shadow protocol after decades of missions together. You are so enthralled, brother, with the prospect of becoming an Elder that you have forgotten how to be the warrior that you still are," I said, in challenge to my brother.

Rather than the expected battle cry or even a growl, Ghorvik remained silent. Moments passed while words slowly came.

"You are correct. I have been more focused on being an Elder than a warrior. I thought to ease the transition for my brothers through acceptance and knowledge, hoping somehow to take the edge off. In the process, my warrior's instincts have been dulled. I did not notice when you enacted the shadow protocol. Perhaps I am not worthy of being the leader of our band," he said reflectively.

"Ghorvik, you have always been as you are now. You often have a myopic view of our missions, focusing primarily on maintaining the ship and our safety. Not much has changed in that regard," I said, in an effort to reassure him.

"Your plan is sound, but we do not need to return to Orcqlaneasus to enact it. We will contact the Directorate and let them know the latest turn of events. A diplomatic mission to secure the future of our world through human mates has long been discussed in the Directorate, especially now with the birth of many Orcqlaneasion sons. Attempting to keep it a secret is a futile task, now that it appears our enemies know that they can ensnare us by taking a human captive."

"Yes, the Gernicians are a menace that has been allowed to persist for too long," Ghorvik said.

"I will contact the Directorate and apprise them of the situation. Later, we will take a stealth shuttle and rendezvous with our brothers at our mate's dwelling. This mission, brother, will be twofold: protect our mate without intruding on her life until she is ready to accept us, and establish a pathway for human females to become mates to Orcqlaneasions."

***

Plotting strategies, navigating thorny missions, and finding solutions to problems yet unknown were all in my area of expertise. But anticipating anything related to my human mate left me at a loss for understanding.

My brothers Chozek and Whorvek had understood the mission far better than Ghorvik. They had purchased our mate passage on a private shuttle and, unbeknownst to her or anyone else for that matter, stowed away, accompanying her on the journey to Earth.

Upon arrival on Earth, she immediately returned to her domicile. Chozek and Whorvek had covertly installed both grid surveillance and security, cloaking our mate's residence and transport in a veil of invisible safety that would protect her while being undetectable to any human, including our mate.

On the ship, Ghorvik contacted the Directorate and held a private vid-conference with the Orcqlaneasion families, our brothers, and me. It should be a simple matter to explain the events following the rescue and have the mission sanctioned by the Directorate.

"Wait a second, you did what?"

The first question by Earth Mother Lydia took my brethren and me by surprise.

Before my brothers or I could answer, a quick response followed from Earth Mother Yvonne as the human females redirected my carefully crafted stratagem with a series of questions and commentaries.

"There's no way, you have to undo it now!"

"Right, you mean she doesn't know you've got her under surveillance."

"I don't know about the rest of y'all, but where I come from, we call that stalking."

"I can't believe I'm saying this, but I agree with Sunni. What you are doing, recording her movements and interactions without her permission and lurking about in the background, is 100% stalker behavior."

I interjected briefly after Earth Mother Evalynne's unwarranted criticism.

"We are not stalking our mate. We are protecting her. She insisted upon returning to Earth, so we implemented standard shadow protocol to ensure her safety."

"Standard shadow protocol. Illbrien, is this really a thing?"

Chief Illbrien Rezz, who was known for being merciless in his decisions, replied stoically to his mate.

"It is part of our standard operating procedure when involved in covert missions in hostile territory."

"Hostile territory!" was yelled in concert by at least two of the eight Earth Mothers present on the vid-call.

"Okay, everyone, let's take a pause. There's a lot to consider here, and not just ethically. You've broken a few dozen laws. How can we make our case to the World Court when, right at this moment, you're in clear violation of at least thirty statutes?"

These words, spoken with authority by Earth Mother J.J. Jackson, calmed the temperaments of the assembly of humans.

"Perhaps it might be better if Vivien or I traveled to Earth to lobby on your behalf. Vivien can use her diplomatic connections, and I can use mine as a former jurist on the World Court."

"No!" "Fuck no!" "I will not allow it." "It is not safe." "You cannot go." "Absolutely not!" "Never!"

This time, the cacophony of dissent came from the Orcqlaneasion mates of Earth Mothers Vivien and J.J.

"Silence, everyone!" bellowed Chief Elder Illbrien. "It has already been well established that gestating mothers put both themselves and their unborn sons at great risk when they are not on Orcqlaneasus, so that is not an option that can be entertained."

"Okay, I understand. I would not want to do anything to endanger my babies, but I am afraid you're not going to get anywhere without our direct intervention," Earth Mother Vivien said.

"As it stands, you have illegally entered Earth space, and you're on the planet in stealth mode. Probably two of the three things that humans fear most." Earth Mother J.J. again lent her legal expertise to our current situation.

"I am curious, beloved, what is the third?" Elder Coervich asked of his mate, when another female answered in her place.

"We fear being eaten, or being enslaved, or being eaten and enslaved, which is way worse, right."

"Sunni, dear, that is not really helping right now," Earth Mother Vivien said calmly.

Earth Mother Sunni responded, "I know, but it is still true."

"Anyway, Sunni is right again. Getting humans to get past their innate fear when you have violated their laws with both your superior technology and physical stature is, quite frankly, going to be an insurmountable task," Earth Mother Vivien explained.

Earth Mother Evalynne, mate to Chief Elder Illbrien and his brothers, and a former private investigator, added more clarity to the cause.

"As soon as I learned who you had rescued on Mars, I began researching her. Dr. Angela Thomas has published volumes on alien cultures. In fact, her work is the basis of much of the foundational knowledge humans have about alien species. She might be able to help you make your case."

"Yeah, she might help you, but there's the whole watching her sleep, eat, work, and go about her whole life under a microscope," Earth Mother Yvonne interjected.

"I saw an old movie like this when I was a kid. I think it was called *The Truman Show*," said Earth Mother Sunni.

"Yes, I know that movie. Very good. Very creepy. The premise was that this person was being watched and recorded. Every second of his life was under scrutiny in real time. It was a dystopian reality show, well before they became an actual thing and got canceled for being too extreme," Earth Mother Thalia said, speaking amongst the assembly for the first time.

"Ladies, I get the idea, but let's get back to the central point. How do we help the Space Orcs negotiate a parlay of sorts with Earth's governments?" Earth Mother Nina said.

"I don't think that you do. Dealing with governments, even the central governing body of the World Court, is going to be a bureaucratic nightmare. Instead, it should be handled as a business negotiation. The Space Orcs are a private entity, and basically, they want to establish an old-fashioned mail-order bride program." The idea of handling our request as a business transaction came from Earth Mother Lydia Collins, a wealthy entrepreneur who still had financial interests on Earth.

"You're right, that's exactly what it's like," said Earth Mother Nina.

I was curious, as were my brothers and most probably the other Orcqlaneasion males, but following our strict protocols, only broken in a moment of anger, only Chief Elder Illbrien and I spoke during this meeting to ensure its brevity and clarity. In the future, someone should apprise the Earth Mothers of our norms.

"Explain this mail-order bride," I said.

"In Earth's history, in what would become the United States, there were more men than women in the western part of the country. To get women, or wives, men would advertise for a wife from the northern states, and generally desperate women who wanted to leave their circumstances would apply. They would correspond by mail a few times, and then the men would pay the travel fare for the women to come to the West, where they would marry them."

"Ooh, that seems like it could have been awful, marrying a complete stranger and living in a strange new place," Earth Mother Sunni said.

"Seriously, did she really just say that? How long did you know your assassins before you wound up here?" Earth Mother Thalia countered.

"Yeah, my bad, but you know what I mean. Back then things were awful, and human men ain't like our Space Orcs even a little bit," Earth Mother Sunni responded.

"Okay, I get your meaning, Sis, but let's workshop this out. If these four Space Orcs cannot convince their mate to come to Orcqlaneasus and create a life with them after being mated to them, it is going to be damn hard to convince Jenny off the block to do the same," Earth Mother Nina stated.

"Well, they're not looking for a Jenny, more like a Tasha or Latoya," Earth Mother Sunni said with unaccountable humor.

"No, maybe someone a little older, like a Natalie or a Nicole," Earth Mother Yvonne said, joining in the odd human humor that only they seemed to understand.

"Good, so we have a task at hand. We will create a business plan to start a private intergalactic mail-order bride system. All you have to do is convince your mate to willingly accept you and help you implement it. If you cannot, though, the whole idea should be shelved. Ladies, do you agree?" Earth Mother Lydia concluded.

"Yep." "I agree." "Me too." "Sounds like a plan." "Sure."

"I think we need to think it through a bit more, and there are several legalities this needs to meet, but I am good if everyone else is."

"I agree with J.J. It will not be an easy sell, but Lydia's idea of making it a private enterprise makes sense."

Chief Elder Illbrien again called for order.

"It seems like the Earth Mothers have a consensus among themselves. I will present this to the Directorate, but I see no objection arising from the plan, assuming, of course, our brothers can complete the mission on their end."

His mate, Earth Mother Evalynne, said, "Illbrien, dear, referring to Shavrek, Ghorvik, Chozek, and Whorvek's task as a mission brings back bad memories and sounds bad too."

"Mercenary." "Cold-blooded." "Heartless." "Calculating," chimed several voices of discontent from the other human females.

Calling for order yet again, Illbrien said, "Enough, I understand. Brothers, cherish the mate that you have been given as we cherish ours. If you are successful in gaining her trust and assuring her of yours, then we will proceed. If not, and I am not being melodramatic as my mate claims, we will cease this endeavor. Take heed, brothers, because our future hinges on your behavior.

# CHAPTER 9: Angela's Homecoming

The first night I got home, I was ecstatic. At least, I felt that way until my head hit the pillow. I had basically survived an alien abduction, being buried alive, and a full-on gang bang. What the absolute fuck.

I wasn't sure which trauma to tackle first, not that the Space Orcs had been traumatic at all. If anything, they were the highlight of my most recent nightmare. Still, I really just wanted to sleep and bury everything that had happened, both the good and the bad, alongside all the other traumas of a lifetime that hovered on the fringes of my nightmares, where my dreams and reality collided.

I couldn't let that happen, though. If I did, I knew the consequences: first a psychotic break, followed by an involuntary stay in a psych ward. Then a series of drug therapies that dumbed my senses to the point that I barely had control of my bodily functions. This is what they called stabilization. The only thing worse was recovery, where I went through the painful process of being detoxed as the drugs slowly left my system.

No matter what, I had to put on a semblance of sanity, enough to fool my colleagues and my department chair, at least.

I knew I was spiraling, especially because my paranoia was in overdrive. Ever since I got home, I kept feeling like I was being watched, like I wasn't alone in my home. My little sanctuary, where I'd always felt at peace, was different somehow. It didn't make me feel safe. If anything, I felt abandoned and alone.

Nighttime was the worst. Fragments of memories from my first near-death encounter merged with my most recent one. But then, just when terror would overtake me, I'd feel surrounded, protected, and my mind would play out the visions of my time with the Space Orcs in vivid detail. Last night, I even woke up, sure that someone or something had touched me in my sleep. I'd been dreaming of having Chozek and Whorvek deep inside me, on the verge of an orgasm, when I swear I felt a clawed hand on my thigh. Of course, when I woke up, no one was there, further solidifying my delusional state.

Today, though, I had to keep my shit together. I had to meet with my department chair and find out if I even had a job left to come back to after my sudden departure to attend a respite center on the other side of the country. At least that's the bullshit excuse I used to access my FMLA and take time off. I hoped no one questioned it too much, given my history, but at the time, I wanted to go so badly I didn't work the whole idea out. Now, though, I had to figure shit out to keep my job.

As an educator, there were a lot of things you could do that, while not best practices, weren't absolutely wrong. But leaving at the start or mid-semester was an unforgivable sin in the eyes of both students and administrators.

I couldn't earn the trust of my students because, first, they were virtual and I'd never untangled that weave. Second, I'd never met them, so they knew as much about me as I knew about them. No, that's not true. They probably knew of my flaky reputation that I'd lived up to by exiting the class without explanation. Lastly, most of them had opted for the in-person option that featured live digs of possible earthly alien encounters, so the handful of students who had registered had simply dropped the class.

As for the administration, my biggest hurdle would be Dickerson. He had expressly forbidden me from having anything to do with the alien mission, and I had jumped on it as soon as possible. I can't say that I had broken his trust, since there was no trust between us to break.

He knew about my past, and each time I'd been institutionalized, it had been at his behest. I never had a lot of family, and once the aunt who raised me died, I lost touch with the few that I did have. Normally, family would take on the responsibility of contacting authorities in a mental health crisis, but Dickerson had assumed the role on his own as my immediate supervisor years ago. I never really questioned it before, but now the weirdness of that, along with everything else, buzzed in my brain.

There was nothing left to do now but face the consequences of my actions. I put off going back to the university to check on my job status for as long as possible, but a week was long enough to hide. Plus, being alone in a paranoid state only made the situation worse, not better.

I got up, got dressed, and tried a positive affirmation in the mirror.

"Okay, girl, you got this. You know what you're going to say. Tell him you were overwhelmed and needed a break. Shit, that's not going to work. He'll see through that in a New York minute. Maybe I should just admit that I took an interview with the alien researchers, and that's all. There's no way he can know I went to Mars, right?"

The pep talk I gave myself didn't work because I still had questions about the whole Mars thing. And thinking about it, and how close I came to almost dying, had me shaking something fierce.

"Get yourself together, Angie! He is the last person you want seeing you have a meltdown."

Maybe yelling at myself didn't do a lot, but it made me feel a little better.

I grabbed my purse and briefcase and left the eerie quiet of my home to face yet another unknown future.

***

As I entered the Anthropology Department's main office, the chairperson's secretary, Maggie, immediately greeted me.

Breathlessly, she said, "Hello, Professor. Dr. Dickerson is expecting you."

She shimmied from behind her desk to escort me to his door, all the while looking at me with uncharacteristic sympathy.

I wondered what that was about, but I set those thoughts aside and walked into his office.

Immediately, I was overcome with a wave of nausea. The pounding of drums beat in wild syncopation at my temple, and my legs gave way.

An arm reached out to steady me, but the scalding touch had me gather my strength and pull away instantly.

Facing me was the nightmare I had not seen in more than two decades. It was my former colleagues Perez and Brett, and our team leader, Ryan.

I physically felt a lock click in my head, and a wave of memories I had never been able to recover came rushing to the forefront.

***

*It was a raucous night. We'd left the lab after getting the news about our selection to lead the alien comm team and had gone on an old-fashioned bar crawl.*

*Nobody was in any condition to drive, so we all piled into an Uber. I remember falling asleep in the car, waking up, and stumbling into Ryan's condo.*

*Even drunk, I remember being amazed by the luxurious apartment. It looked like something out of a magazine, with floor-to-ceiling windows and a 360-degree view of downtown.*

*That was really the first realization I had, albeit belatedly, that I was someplace I shouldn't be and out of my element.*

*Ryan's wealth was apparent in every nook and corner of where he lived, and I wasn't the only one who noticed.*

*"What the fuck, boss, you living like this?" Perez said, slurring his words, indicating he was just as drunk as I was.*

*"Yeah, right. I keep thinking you are one of us, but this is like Cribs on steroids," he said, referencing an old MTV show that constantly ran on repeat on the free TV channels.*

*Ryan seemed annoyed and said, "Shut the fuck up, you plebe. There are rooms down the hall. Find one and sleep it off."*

*I assumed he meant me too and started to follow the other two, but Ryan grabbed my hand.*

*"Not you. I've got a place for you to crash." He pulled me in close and kissed me.*

*I eagerly returned his kiss, even though my inebriated brain was sending out warning signs I chose to ignore.*

*He pushed open his bedroom door, and I was struck by how tricked out his place was. My instincts screamed, "You don't belong here!" But I silenced them when I felt Ryan grab my ass and shove me onto the bed.*

*"Okay, you don't have to be rough, baby. I'm down for whatever," I said, trying to get a little more control of the situation as I lifted myself up on my elbows. I was a little surprised by his behavior, especially since he was the prototypical mild-mannered professor. But I was more worried about the last time my kitty had been trimmed. Since I was so busy at work, with no man in sight, shaving or waxing wasn't on the agenda.*

*Abruptly breaking my thoughts, Ryan said, "Shut the fuck up and take what I give you."*

*My fuzzy brain snapped clear in an instant, and I was sober as a judge. I leaped off the bed.*

*"Who the fuck do you think you're talking to?" I yelled back.*

*"Don't try and act like a saint, Angela. Everybody knows what a whore you are," he sneered.*

*Clear-eyed, I sized him up and wondered what I'd ever seen in him. I got up in his face and said, "Fuck you!"*

*I pushed past him to walk out the bedroom door, and he grabbed my arm, twisting it behind my back.*

*"That's the plan, Angela," he said, grabbing my face in his free hand as I tried to swing at him with my fist. "What, you didn't think I noticed your lame attempts at flirting with me? I ignored it at first, because I don't go for Black chicks, but how many times was I supposed to walk past that fat ass you kept flashing at me?"*

*I tried to wrench away, realizing Ryan was a lot stronger than he appeared. I was cussing and swearing at him to release me, all the while he was laughing like a maniac.*

*He pushed me back down on the bed and dove on top of me. This time, there was nothing sexy or romantic about it, and I could smell the alcohol on him that I hadn't noticed before.*

*I heard what sounded like a quick knock at the bedroom door and saw Perez and Brett rush in.*

*"What the fuck is going on?" Brett asked in a drunken stupor.*

*Perez asked another equally dumb-ass question, "Is this where the party is?"*

*Perez rushed forward. I thought, maybe, just maybe, he would help me, but all hope soon died.*

*"Oh yeah, I want to get a piece of this uppity bitch," he said.*

*Ryan moved to the left as Perez jumped onto the bed on the right, and I used that change in position to lift my leg and land a solid blow to his balls.*

*Ryan yelped and doubled over, falling off the bed. I pushed Perez off me, which was relatively easy since he was skinny and lanky and I was a much bigger girl, with size and anger on my side.*

*I made it off the bed, with Perez struggling to get up on the right and Ryan still crumpled over on the left. Unfortunately, I didn't see Brett and figured he must have left the chaos, wanting no part of it.*

*I figured wrong. Just as my hand reached the doorknob, I felt glass and liquid splinter across the back of my head. My knees buckled, and I gave in to the pain, succumbing to a wave of darkness.*

*The next sensation I felt was icy coldness. I was wrapped tight in something, maybe a thick blanket or comforter. My face was sticky with what I had to believe was blood. My head ached, and my voice was trapped by the fear of the moment. I heard disjointed voices around me, and I struggled to make out what I was hearing.*

*"Steve, what took you so long to get here?" It sounded like Ryan, but the voice was too muffled to make it out clearly. He was talking to someone who wasn't Perez or Brett, so maybe I could get some help.*

*"I got here as fast as I fucking could," the unknown male voice said. "Where the fuck is she?"*

*"We wrapped her in the Persian rug from the den."*

*"Your mother is going to shit bricks when she sees that her rug is missing."*

*"I don't give a fuck about her rug. I just want to get rid of the body."*

*Body, were they talking about me? I wanted to scream, I'm not dead, I'm not dead, but no words came out as I felt a steady flow of liquid congeal at the corner of my lips. I tried to stay conscious, but I couldn't.*

*The next time I woke up, it was cold and wet. Everything hurt, and I was still wrapped tightly in the fucking rug.*

*I heard voices again, but I was still too weak to cry out, and my instincts, which I was finally listening to, told me to keep my mouth closed.*

*"We should have taken her to the Everglades. They find bodies of indigents off Alligator Alley every other week, and nobody gives a fuck," Ryan said.*

*"I don't want to drive that fucking far. A fucking canal in the hood gets the same result. They'll just think she's another nameless nigger whore. I'm more worried about those two," the strange voice, I think he said his name was Steve, said.*

*"They'll be fine. Neither of them wanted her on the mission. They fucking complained about her every day. Plus, Perez would've fucked her if Brett hadn't killed her first. They've got more to lose than I do."*

*"Fine. You two, get out of the truck and help us off-load this fat bitch, then get out of here."*

*I felt the sensation of being lifted, and as much as I wanted to kick and fight, my body was frozen, wracked with pain and fear.*

*Then I heard Perez say clearly, "This bitch weighs a ton."*

*Followed by Brett, "No doubt."*

*"Wait, your mother's fancy-ass rug is identifiable. Roll her out of it and shove her fat ass in the canal."*

*There was a sharp kick to my side, another to my back, and still another to my stomach. My eyes were swollen, sealed shut by the blood that oozed from my head wound.*

***

Memories of the final, painful kick to my head pulled me out of my past, and for the first time in twenty-eight years, I remembered exactly what happened to me.

It felt like a dark, heavy veil had been lifted from my mind, and all my disjointed memories finally clicked into place.

The uncomfortable sensation whenever I was around my department chair, Steve Dickerson, finally made sense as I realized he was an accomplice to my attempted murder. Worse yet, he'd offered me a job, helped my career, and whenever things went spiraling out of control, arranged for my sabbaticals in the psych ward.

It was like a faucet had been turned on, and all the past came rushing back. But I wasn't broken or scared this time. I realized how these men had conspired and failed to take my life, but then manipulated my mind, my career, and my very existence for almost three decades.

Backing away from them toward the door, the words spilled from my lips.

"I know. I know what you did to me. I remember everything. It was the night we found out about the mission. We were drinking, and ended up back at your place. You took me to your bedroom, got rough, and when I tried to get away, you pushed me down and tried to rape me."

I didn't realize I'd been pointing at Ryan the entire time until I saw Perez smirking at me.

"You were a part of it too. You tried to hold me down, but I fought my way away from both of you. Then Brett hit me, and I passed out.

You tried to kill me. You called for help to dump me in a canal in my old neighborhood. Somehow, when I hit the water, I was able to swim to shore, and a rush of water from the sewer dump pushed me away before you checked to see if I was dead.

I pulled myself up to the shore, and eventually I was found alive, not dead like you'd planned. But I couldn't remember what happened, just bits and pieces.

Y'all made up some story that I left the bar on my own and probably went to my old dives on Sistrunk, where I ran into somebody who attacked me. It didn't make sense to me, but I kept thinking it was possible.

But it was all a lie, and you've all conspired against me this whole time, making me think I was insane."

In a rage, I screamed. Maybe Maggie would hear me and call for help.

"Keep going, Angela. Nobody is going to believe you after all this time. It'll just be another psychotic break that you probably won't even remember. Perez, Brett, grab her," Ryan said, issuing orders like in times past, with the other two following blindly.

"After this dose of psychotropic drugs starts circulating in your system, you'll be hallucinating little green men in space suits flying on unicorns."

Dickerson stopped Ryan before he could administer the drug.

"Wait, I want to know how you got off Mars. When the Gernicians contacted Ryan and me to provide a Black human female for a substantial sum of money, no questions asked, we thought we'd be free of you forever. How the fuck did you survive? You were supposed to be bait in an alien honeytrap."

I was pulling and trying to get away from Brett and Perez's hold.

"Fuck you!" I yelled, and Brett slapped me so hard across the cheek my neck whipped back and my vision faltered. At first, I saw white spots, and then, as my vision cleared, I saw the office explode into a million fragments as dust, wood, and plaster flew through the air.

Instantly, I felt the hold of Brett and Perez give way, and as the dust settled, I felt my back pressed against a strong wall of solid flesh, a green, muscled forearm wrapped around my midsection, holding me in place.

Impossible as it was for me to believe they were here, rescuing me once more, they were my Space Orcs. Chozek was on my left, Whorvek was on my right. From the deep scars that ran along his arms, I knew that I was being held by Ghorvik, while Shavrek stood in front of me.

I looked around the chaos of the room and saw Brett, bleeding and clutching a limb that looked almost completely severed from his body. Perez was in the corner, cowering in fright, bloody and bruised, while both Ryan and Steve had been knocked the fuck out, each with vivid red claw marks across their necks and torsos.

In just seconds, the Space Orcs had shredded my former captors with almost lethal blows, using just their bare hands, well, claws.

I was completely caught up in the carnage my mates had created. The office was in shambles, with the unconscious, hopefully dead, bodies of Ryan and Steve sprawled across the desk and floor. Unfortunately, Brett and Perez were still very much alive, as evidenced by the whimpers and cries coming from the corner where they tried to hide.

They disgusted me, and my thoughts turned darker and darker as their abuse played over and over in my mind. I was spiraling in anger and pain when Shavrek's raspy voice brought me back.

"Anjua, are you hurt?" He gently brought his clawed hand to my chin and lifted my face, touching the raised welt that Brett had inflicted just moments earlier.

Still amazed that they were actually here, I found my words that had momentarily escaped me.

"I'm good now. Why are you here? How did you find me?"

Shavrek said, "We are here because we never left you."

"What, wait, are you even supposed to be here?" I stared again at the chaotic scene around me. As much as I wholeheartedly approved, I knew this shit was going to be the cause of an intergalactic incident.

"We are supposed to be with our mate. We would never leave you alone on such a hostile, violent planet, even if it is your homeworld," Chozek said by way of explanation.

"Okay, I get it, but maybe we should leave. I know how the authorities can be. I wouldn't want them to take you into custody over this."

At that, each of my mates laughed heartily. I finally realized, hell yeah, they were my mates. They showed up for me, live and in person, and brought justice with them.

Ghorvik wrapped both arms around me tightly and kissed the top of my head. He then said, "You are correct, Anjua. We have no wish to injure others of your species. Chozek, engage the portal generator back to the shuttle."

Chozek pulled out a small device and pointed it at one of the office walls that had remained undisturbed in the squabble. The wall seemed to fold into itself as an opening appeared.

I was still staring in awe at the alien technology, with a million questions at the tip of my tongue, when Ghorvik swooped me up into his arms, carrying me toward the portal.

"Close your eyes, Anjua. It will be bright," he said as he followed Shavrek into the alien void.

Even though I wanted to see, I thought it better to listen in this instance.

In seconds, we were all in a shuttlecraft similar to the one Chozek and Whorvek had used when they rescued me from Mars.

This time, though, I wasn't confined to a med pod and got to see more of space than I had in all my recent journeys. I sat in a seat and got a firsthand view of Earth from space.

In that moment, I quietly reflected on the revelations I'd just uncovered prior to my rescue. My colleagues, my supervisors, had all conspired to kill me over a hook-up turned sexual assault gone wrong.

Having failed, they had spent decades pulling the strings on my life from the shadows. My psych episodes weren't random. They were orchestrated. By exploiting my very real chronic depression, they created an image of me as high-strung and prone to psychosis. They made sure no one would ever believe the truth, even if by some miracle I remembered it.

Hell, I wouldn't have believed it either if I hadn't confronted them myself.

As we left Earth's surface, I could only assume we were headed back to the moon, since that was where their ship was, the one I had departed from. It didn't matter to me, though. Any place was better than where I'd come from.

I glanced around the small bridge and caught each of my mates staring at me. I smiled, and each one smiled in return. Wherever they were going, I was going with them.

I'd spent my whole career in pursuit of learning about ancient alien civilizations, and now I'd have a firsthand opportunity to live in an alien culture.

I felt like everything would be alright, and I hadn't had that sense of surety since before my attack. And that attack, as bad as it was, would have been nothing compared to what my former colleagues had in store for me.

If the Space Orcs hadn't intervened, I hated to imagine how different my fate would have been. Instead of embarking on a new life on a distant planet, I'd be catatonic in a psychiatric facility, possibly forever, or until I had an unfortunate drug interaction. I felt a chill just thinking about it.

Still, the timing of the Space Orcs' intervention was uncanny, and even though I didn't want to, it was a loose thread I was going to pull.

I waited until the shuttle was back on the ship before I addressed my concerns, because I needed answers before I left everything behind.

Instead of going back to my assigned stateroom, I stayed on the bridge with my mates.

Each one had a station where they posted up, leaving me to sit in what appeared to be a separate section, maybe for guests or visitors.

I was mentally preparing myself for the upcoming conversation when the comms system lit up like a Christmas tree.

Ghorvik said, "Fuck, it is Chief Elder Illbrien. Whorvek, send those fucking vids to him before I respond."

Whorvek shook his head and said, "Fuck, I was hoping we had more time."

"No such luck," Chozek chimed in.

"What's going on?" I asked, pushing my previous questions away.

"The leader of our planetary government is contacting us, most likely about the incident that occurred at the university."

"Oh no, are y'all gonna be in trouble over me?" I asked, concerned.

"Absolutely not. You are our mate. You may even carry our sons now," Shavrek said.

"Um, I hate to break it to you, but as much as I kind of like the idea of being your mate, I'm well past the age of childbearing. Plus, my equipment was faulty even when it did work, so I'm sorry, that's not going to happen," I said, trying to soften the blow.

The comms lights went dark, leaving just one blinking intermittently.

"Anjua, would you like to find out with one hundred percent certainty that you carry our sons?" Shavrek asked.

Whorvek, who was stationed at comms, beckoned me over. Smiling, I approached him and stood between his legs as he sat at his station. He pulled out a small device and pressed a few invisible controls.

"This will detect the new lives growing inside you. We are told it works like a sensitive ultrasound device and will be able to detect the gestational sacs of our younglings. Do you give your consent to use it?" he asked.

I nodded, and he lifted my blouse from my skirt and began to unbutton it. I was so focused on my proximity to him and how my body was already reacting that I didn't notice at first that Chozek slipped in behind me. It wasn't until I felt his clawed hands cup my breasts that I realized he was there.

"You three, let us see if our seed has taken root before you forget the task set before you," Ghorvik grumbled.

Whorvek pressed the small device against my belly, and I brushed Chozek's claws away, pulling my bra back down and stuffing my giant boobs back into the cups.

Again, I was distracted with the task of repackaging the girls in their harness, so I was taken aback when Ghorvik spoke.

"Ah, I see them there. Four small sacs. Our sons."

"What? That's impossible. How is this possible?" I said, staring at the screen and the small life sacs displayed.

"Whatever pheromone cocktail the Pstoadys cooked up is, by all accounts, one hundred percent effective," Shavrek said.

I leaned on Whorvek heavily, staring at him in disbelief. Suddenly, Chozek lifted me up and started carrying me across the bridge.

"This is quite a lot for our mate to process, especially after earlier events today. I will take her to her cabin and make sure she rests," he said, giving me a conspiratorial smile.

As confused as I was, whenever I was in Chozek's arms, my thoughts immediately turned to desire, and that might just be the stress relief I needed to help me "process" everything.

But as much as I wanted sex right now, my brain was on overdrive, and sexual stimulation might just be too much.

As if hearing my thoughts, Ghorvik responded, "Chozek, put her down. We have left many things unsaid with our new mate that we must address to move forward as a thriving bound unit."

Chozek reluctantly put me back in my seat, far from the others on the bridge. As soon as he turned his back, Whorvek beckoned me to come back to him, and I rushed to sit on his lap at his station.

The comms lit up again, and this time the larger video monitor flickered to life with the image of a regal, white-haired Space Orc that I assumed to be Chief Illbrien, as he had been called earlier.

"Greetings, brethren. Is your mate with you?" he asked.

Whorvek adjusted the screen and internal camera so that it showed all of us on the bridge, me included, sitting on his lap.

"We have reviewed the vid from the university, and your actions have been deemed justifiable by the Directorate. The humans wish to hold an inquest, but based on the irrefutable evidence, we feel the Galactic Alliance will agree with us. Your mate is a citizen of Orcqlaneasus and holds the rights and privileges accorded to her. Does she carry your legacy?"

Ghorvik responded, "Yes, Chief Elder. Our mate carries four Orcqlaneasion younglings."

"Excellent. I would suggest, then, that you return with all due haste. Breeding mothers fare much better here than any other place. Laneasus herself embraces them and their babes in her healing waters," he said.

"As for the other matter, if the humans choose to pursue a public inquest, then we will have no choice but to acknowledge our recent change in status. We are no longer the last of the Orcqlaneasions. Thanks to the human females, and yes, Pstoady intervention, we are able to reproduce and repopulate our planet."

"Oh my God, what happened to the Pstoadys? I completely forgot about them," I said out loud and immediately covered my mouth with my hand, thinking I had made some type of cultural faux pas by speaking to their supreme leader.

"Dr. Angela Thomas, on behalf of all Orcqlaneasus, I welcome you and thank you for your duty in delivering the next generation of Orcqlaneasion warriors," he said formally.

I was a little taken aback when a tall, dark-skinned sister with a short, cropped afro appeared next to the Chief Elder.

"Dammit, Illbrien, you're gonna freak the woman out with all that talk about duty to make warriors. Hi, I'm Evalynne Browne, and

Illbrien, Rektrion, and Fraebrion are my mates. I understand that you're a cultural anthropologist, so you should know that some of the alien customs may seem strange to us. Just know Orcqlaneasus is a beautiful, rich, healthy planet.

And once you get here, especially after you bathe in the healing waters, you'll feel the connection and never want to leave. You already know a little something about the Space Orcs since you're already knocked up, but besides that, they are excellent protectors, and they love and nurture their little ones like nobody's business.

Including myself, there are eight other human women here, all sisters of one kind or another. Most of us are middle-aged plus, although I think I'm the oldest. And yes, if it looks like I'm pregnant, I am, and yes, I'm over sixty.

I think that's it for now. Safe travels, and we can't wait to meet you and welcome you to Orcqlaneasus."

She stepped away, and the Chief Elder was about to speak when she returned to the screen.

"Oh, by the way, the Pstoadys are with y'all on the moon, holed up in their freaky little spa. It seems like they were too afraid to go anywhere else, and they want to come back here to Orcqlaneasus."

Chief Elder Illbrien blustered, "Absolutely not, Evalynne. How do you know this? It matters not. The Pstoadys are to be held off planet." The audio for the monitor went mute as we watched Evalynne speak with Chief Illbrien and her two mates.

After an uncomfortable couple of minutes, the sound returned.

"Pick up the Pstoadys and return them to our Alpha moon. The Directorate will determine their final placement once they are here and secured. Safe travels," he said, and the screen went black.

Chozek said, "Never would I have expected Chief Illbrien to be so amenable to the Pstoadys."

"Especially since at one time he had a bounty on their heads to be captured dead or alive," Whorvek replied.

For my part, I was still digesting the whole call. I mean, I was glad the Pstoadys were okay, since they had been instrumental in saving my life, but one thing was still bothering me: the university vids.

"Is someone going to explain how the chaos in Dickerson's office is on vid? And don't tell me that the university recorded it, because I know for a fact the offices don't have recording devices in them."

There was silence, and that never boded well.

"Look, if we're going to be together, we can't have secrets. I've had a lifetime of those. I refuse to let them cloud another moment of whatever time I have left to live."

Shavrek stepped from his station and stood in front of me. He started speaking, and I was afraid of what I was going to hear.

"When you left us on the moon to return to Earth with Chozek and Whorvek, they went with you, unbeknownst to you. They followed and installed security cameras throughout to make sure you were safe while you were away from us. We could not leave you unprotected, and at the time you did not want to be with us, so it was our solution."

Ghorvik left his perch at the captain's chair and walked over to me, continuing the explanation. "Since we made that choice, we were admonished by the human mates on our planet that it was wrong, that it violated your privacy. We had planned to make our presence known to you at some point, once you had restarted your life on Earth, but we could never have foretold how events would unfold," Ghorvik said.

Chozek kneeled down in front of me, and he and Whorvek each lifted one of my limp hands, both waiting anxiously to see what verdict I would deliver based on this new revelation that they had been constantly spying on me.

It rankled me that they had secretly watched me, but if they hadn't done it, I'd be in a mental hospital or worse right now. Still, after a lifetime of deception, could I forgive them for this betrayal?

"Tell me this, did you visit me at night, like when I was asleep? I felt like I wasn't alone. Was that you?"

Chozek responded first. "It was me. I could not stay away from you. I went against my brothers' wishes, but you are all that I think about."

"He is not alone in this. I too went against the wishes of my brothers to remain distant from you. I could feel your restlessness in your dreams. We all could. We are your mates. I tried to shelter you from the negative thoughts, and the best way to do it was up close. Once, I did touch your limb without consent, and for that I am filled with remorse," Whorvek confessed.

I looked at the other two Space Orcs angrily glaring at Chozek and Whorvek, and I laughed. Admittedly, it wasn't the emotion I expected to come bubbling forth, but it did nonetheless.

"You guys are knuckleheads, and for that matter, so am I. You shouldn't have let me go that easily, and I'm still pretty pissed about that. But knowing that you were trying to keep me safe and protected while giving me space is very stalker-like, but also very appreciated. Don't get me wrong, I hate imagining that you saw everything that I did. Did you see everything, like in the bathroom too?" I asked.

"Yes, we saw everything, even your tiny device in the furniture next to your bed that you used to bring yourself to orgasm."

"Oh my God, do you mean my rabbit?" I asked, embarrassed.

"Yes, we saw, and in the spirit of truthfulness, I destroyed the offensive device," Shavrek said, surprising not only me but his bound brothers too.

"What did the rabbit do to you?" I asked, laughing.

Shavrek walked forward a few more steps, not like a man or even an alien, but like a predator stalking his prey. His brothers moved away as if he might pounce on me.

Quietly, he rasped close to my throat, "It was lodged deep within you, your thighs clutched tight. Only cock, tongue, or claw belongs in you, that of mine and my brethren."

"You are ours as we are yours. We will always protect you, whether you want us to or not. This is our culture. This is our vow. Do you accept us? Shall we put this time behind us and move forward in clarity and truth, free of deception and artifice?"

Truth, forgiveness, clarity, forward movement, I wasn't familiar with any of that. Everything in my life had been shrouded in the darkness of deceit. Years of depression, sadness, and stints locked away, drugged and alone, had almost broken me, but not quite.

Maybe I survived it all to be with them.

I wasn't sure what to do, but everything in me felt like I should go with them. Like all my life I had studied, learned, and loved everything about alien cultures, and now it was my time to fully embrace my place in one.

Plus, according to them, I was pregnant. That still didn't feel real. Maybe, given everything that had just happened, my brain just wasn't ready to process it yet.

"Okay, I'm willing to forgive you, because you saved my ass, and supposedly got me pregnant, and y'all know you fine as fuck, but no more secrets, ever, or..."

"Or what, little Anjua, what will you do?" Shavrek asked, menacingly close to me.

"I'll have Chozek and Whorvek kick your ass. And that goes for you too, Ghorvik, because I just know you two set everything up and they just went along with it. Moving forward, let's try to change that dynamic, okay. Let's all be equal partners, even as we each have our own role to play in our bond."

Whorvek whispered loudly so his brethren could hear, "Shall we go back to our cabin and consummate our new bond, Anjua?" he asked.

"Absolutely not. Let's get those fucking Pstoadys and put this whole solar system behind us. I'm eager to get to your homeworld."

"It is yours too, Anjua," Chozek said.

"Oh yeah, why do you guys keep mispronouncing my name? Angie is short for Angela, not Anjua."

"No, Anjua means cherished, beloved, protected. It is an archaic term that fell from use when our females perished, but it shows how we feel about you."

"Alright, I like it then. Hell, I love it. Come on, I'm ready for my life to start on Orcqlaneasus."

# EPILOGUE: An End to the Experiment

"The Space Orcs have arrived."

"Yes, they are finally here."

"Everything we need is packed and secure."

"Yes, we have everything required to run our final experiment."

"Everything except our final test subject."

"Yes, we are still missing our final human to complete the experiment."

"I wonder if we should proceed."

"Perhaps we should not."

"I am unsure what to do."

"As am I."

"We should ask most adored Dr. Nina Bridges how we should proceed."

"Yes, we should contact her immediately."

"But we cannot."

"No, we cannot."

"She has many, many responsibilities."

"Even more than when she was our most cherished Director."

"Of course, you are wise to remember."

"Yes, I remember."

"She created vid instructions to guide us when we did not know what to do."

"Or when there were too many casualties to attend."

"Yes, she had many, many responsibilities then as well."

"Computer, access Med-Space-Gamma 7 scientific training log, lesson 912."

"Yes, Computer, access lesson 912.4, procedural instruction by Dr. Nina Bridges."

The wall of the defunct original Moon Dust Spa and Salon sparked to life. A wall-sized image of Dr. Nina Bridges appeared. The recording date indicated a time eight years earlier, during the height of the Distant Wars.

*"Hello, Torvak. Hello, Tovak. Today I want to answer the question you posed about whether you must complete all planned experiments once you obtain results that support your hypothesis.*

*First, evidence is important. One experiment that supports your hypothesis is rarely enough to draw a valid conclusion. You still need replication, controls, statistical significance, and confirmation through different methods.*

*Second, there are ethical considerations. Sometimes it's not necessary to continue an experiment if doing so would be unnecessary, wasteful, dangerous, or even ethically questionable.*

*Third, early positive results can sometimes prove misleading due to bias, chance, sample size, or variables you can't control.*

*I know this is a little confusing to you both, so let's think about it this way. The scientific method isn't about rigidly completing every planned step no matter what. It's about gathering enough reliable evidence to justify a conclusion."*

*A klaxon alarm blared through the recording, and Dr. Bridges glanced away, distracted.*

*"Okay, we have a new ship of wounded warriors arriving. I've got to go. I'm sorry I haven't had more time to help you better understand the scientific method and process.*

*But both of you are doing an incredible job, and there are no scientists I would rather have on my team than you two.*

*Talk to you later."*

The wall screen vanished as though it had never existed.

"What a wise idea to seek adored Dr. Nina Bridges' advice."

"Yes, her guidance is always sound."

"We should have consulted the vids long ago."

"Exactly, she has given us our answer."

"Yes," in unison. "We will proceed."

# ABOUT THE AUTHOR

**Solar Black** is a passionate and imaginative writer who masterfully blends romance, fantasy, and science fiction, carving out a unique space in the genre by centering Black women as lead characters in thrilling alien romances. Her stories feature mature, adventurous heroines who find themselves entangled in high-stakes adventures and passionate, often reverse harem relationships with powerful alien warriors.

With a signature style that fuses epic action, deep emotional connections, and sensual, erotic moments, Solar captivates readers by bringing to life richly detailed worlds filled with danger, desire, and destiny. Whether it's the fierce and noble Orcqlaneasions or the enigmatic and seductive Snakemen of Nyokaa, her alien warriors are as complex as they are captivating, facing battles for survival, love, and redemption. From cosmic wars to intimate struggles of the heart, Solar's stories promise exhilarating journeys where romance is just as intense as the battles waged across galaxies.

For more information visit: **www.solarblackboard.com**

# SERIES BY AUTHOR

## THE LAST OF THE ORCQLANEASIONS

In a distant galaxy, ***The Last of the Orcqlaneasions*** series chronicles the dwindling population of giant alien warriors. These formidable beings are the toughest in all the galaxies, feared by their enemies and revered by their allies.

Bound brothers of two, three, or four form unbreakable bonds and search for the one thing that can save their kind, a mate. Without women to complete their unit, carry their young, and share their life force, their species teeters on the brink of extinction.

With every passing day, their numbers decrease, and their hope for survival wanes. Desperate for a solution, they scour the universe, seeking the rarest and most treasured of all, Black women. Not only capable of bearing their offspring, these women possess the resilience, intelligence, and fire to stand beside them as equals.

Despite their fierce reputation, the Orcqlaneasions are willing to risk everything for their mates. To them, these women are not just a means of survival; they are their heart, their future, their salvation.

The warriors vow to love, protect, and devote themselves completely, forging a bond stronger than war, time, or fate itself.

## Space Orcs and the Director – Book 1

At the end of the Distant Wars, Med-Space Gamma-7 is set to close. Dr. Nina Bridges, the human director from Earth, faces an uncertain future alongside her security team, four fierce Orcqlaneasions, the last of their dwindling species. Kaelix Voss, Talix Krynn, Zephix Jorin, and Aerix Thorne, each a towering warrior with a powerful presence, find themselves drawn to Nina in a bond fueled by overwhelming passion and a desperate desire to ensure the survival of their kind. As they navigate the aftermath of the wars, will they overcome their differences and find lasting love, or will their turbulent pasts and ingrained distrust keep them apart? In this tale of desire and destiny, the stakes are higher than ever.

## Space Orcs and the Thief – Book 2

Thalia Montgomery, a former space marine turned mercenary, is stranded on the dangerous moon of KX-7. In a fight for survival, she encounters two Pstoadys scientists with a wild request. They need her to pull off a heist from a nearby wrecked ship.

The problem is, the ship belongs to three powerful Orcqlaneasion warriors. Gorak Malak, Thargok Vorr, and Varnok Zenn are battle-hardened brothers with one goal in mind, finding a mate to secure the future of their kind. When they review their surveillance footage, they discover Thalia, a bold and resourceful human who stirs something deeper than anger.

Is she the answer they've been waiting for, or just a thief chasing her next payday?

## Space Orcs and the Pilot – Book 3

Yvonne Adams, an attractive ebony-skinned woman and former colonist on Nu-Terra, lost everything in a brutal alien attack. Her family was taken, and the four Orcqlaneasion warriors meant to protect them never came. Now, years later, she makes her way as a salvage ship operator, surviving in the silence of deep space.

But fate has other plans. Yvonne comes face to face with the warriors she blames for her loss. As old wounds resurface, so do questions of guilt, forgiveness, and desire. Can they earn her trust, or is the damage too deep to mend?

This is a story of survival, heartbreak, and the search for healing in the unlikeliest of places.

**Trigger Warning**: This story contains references to child loss, late-term miscarriage, and alien abduction. Reader discretion is advised.

## Space Orcs and the Diplomat – Book 4

Vivien Johnson, a brilliant African American diplomat once celebrated across the Galactic Alliance, now lives in quiet exile after the massacre on Nu-Terra. Forced into retirement, her only connection to her former life is her niece, Dr. Nina Bridges. But when Nina vanishes without a trace, Vivien emerges from hiding to uncover the truth.

Her search leads her deep into Orcqlaneasion space, where the Directorate Elders rule with wisdom earned through war. Once fearsome warriors, now advisors and protectors, these giants weigh her presence carefully. Some view her with suspicion, others with cautious hope, but all recognize the threat she poses to tradition.

As Vivien confronts her past and challenges ancient customs, she must decide how far she'll go to reunite her family. For the Elders, it may be their last chance to fight for a future worth living.

## Space Orcs and the CEO – Book 5

Lydia Collins-Adler, once the powerful CEO of Lunar Dynamics, lost everything in a bitter divorce. Bankrupt and banned from starting over on Earth, she flees to the stars in search of a second chance and answers about the disappearance of her mentor, Ambassador Vivien Johnson.

Her journey brings her face to face with four Orcqlaneasion warriors: Xarufh, Parnifh, Jaraefh, and Veltrufh. They're investigating a rumored human conspiracy that could jeopardize the future of Orcqlaneasus. When they encounter Lydia, they see more than a mystery. They see a potential threat.

Desire pulls them together, but suspicion simmers beneath the surface. Can Lydia be trusted, or will her presence endanger the fragile prospects for a species on the brink of extinction?

## Space Orcs and the Investigator – Book 6

Chief Elder Illbrien Rezz is a leader unraveling. His rule is faltering, his brotherhood is broken, and his grip on sanity is slipping. The Orcqlaneasions stand at a crossroads, caught between the promise of human mates and the chaos stirred by two meddling Pstoady scientists.

Retired investigator Evalynne Browne is called back into action to track down the Pstoadys. Known for her dogged determination and no-nonsense demeanor, she expects a mission. What she finds instead is Illbrien, a man consumed by obsession, who believes Evalynne is the key to saving his brotherhood and restoring his fractured mind.

But nothing is as it seems, and as they fight together on a hostile planet, his obsession may lead to an untimely death or an unexpected new life.

## Space Orcs and the Cosmetologist – Book 7

Sunni Davis always has a smile, but losing her home, her business, and her man left her with little to be cheerful about. A new job offer at the exclusive Moon Dust Spa and Salon on Earth's moon seems like a dream come true.

But things are not what they seem. The spa hides a secret, and when Sunni makes a desperate choice, she ends up in the crosshairs of four Orcqlaneasion elite assassins sent to bring her in.

Now she's on the run. Can she escape their pursuit, or will she fall into their claws?

## Space Orcs and the Judge – Book 8

Judge Judith Jiminez-Jackson thought she was done with conflict.

She left the World Court behind, buried her husband, and took on small cases in peace, only to be pushed out of the law firm she built by her scheming stepsons.

When a familiar interstellar client calls in a favor, she has no choice but to answer or risk losing everything she has spent a lifetime building. Facing her fears, she travels to the snake planet of Nyokaa and walks straight into treachery and deception.

Can she trust the Elder Space Orcs who claim to be helping her? Or has she uncovered a dark interplanetary trafficking ring where humans are drugged and bred by aliens?

Haunted by fear, grief, and betrayal, Judith must let go of the past and confront the truth of her present situation to claim a future she never imagined.

## Space Orcs and the Professor – Book 9

Professor Angela Thomas has spent a lifetime questioning her own mind.

After surviving a near-death experience she cannot explain, she stopped trusting herself. Still, when one last opportunity comes to chase the future she once believed was hers, she takes it, only to discover it was a trap not meant for her, but for the Space Orcs.

The Space Orcs are preparing for ascension into the Directorate, stepping into a future that will reshape Orcqlaneasus and secure the survival of their people. Their final mission was never supposed to include her, yet they find her anyway, pulling her back from the brink and into a connection none of them wanted or planned.

Will Angela return to the life she knows, and can the Space Orcs move forward without her, or has everything already changed?

# SERIES BY AUTHOR

## THE SNAKEMEN OF NYOKAA

**Dukari: An AMBW K-pop Alien Romance**

***Kayla's K-pop dreams become reality, with an alien twist.***

Kayla Thomas Milgram's Seoul vacation takes an unexpected turn when she encounters Dukari, an alien stranded on Earth who looks uncannily like her middle school K-pop idol. His infamous disguise quickly attracts unwanted attention, sparking a series of chaotic misadventures.

As Dukari helps Kayla confront her fears, she introduces him to the complexities of humanity. Realizing they are true mates, their connection deepens, but Kayla begins to wonder if Dukari is hiding more than just his true identity. With surprises, deception, sabotage, and secrets threatening to unravel everything, their love is tested in ways neither of them expected.

Slink into the seductive and thrilling world of Dukari, the tantalizing prequel to the upcoming Snakemen of Nyokaa series.

Also available in Audiobook.

# ACKNOWLEDGMENTS

Thank you to my friends, family, supporters, and yes, even the haters. Each of you played a role in shaping the crazy, other-worldly stories I create.

My educator mentor, Smith, read my work with a literary eye and never let me settle. Now my most honest critic, you pushed me to write narratives that can stand on their own, with or without the heat.

To the fierce young people I had the honor of teaching, nearly twenty five years in your lives changed me. I am deeply proud of you, and I carry your brilliance and resilience with me into this next chapter.

My roots began with my folks, the Turners. You taught me how to be a loving parent, and though you left me as I was just becoming a young adult, those lessons became the blueprint I used to nurture and love my two extraordinary children.

Speaking of my children, Renny and Rissy, you are the foundation of my life. Your unconditional love has sustained me, and your undaunted bravery has inspired me. My son reminded me that it was not too late to chase my dream of writing, and my daughter embraced my work without judgment or criticism. I pushed you to follow your dreams, and you turned around and pushed me to follow mine.

I have been carried by my sisterhood of friends and my Sorority sisters, especially those who stood by me when I could not stand for myself.

My social media crew, Storm, Shannon, Nicole, Natalie, Cocoa, Alexis, E. Tasha, Monet, and Toni, showed up for me in real ways. Alongside them are the authors who inspired me and my Facebook family of Intergalactic Black Love.

Special thanks to Ta'Nai Reign for being the best assist at book events, and to my big bro' DeWayne for showing up and supporting me in person.

I am truly blessed beyond all measure, and yes, I will thank God in all that I do.

Love y'all,
Solar Black

www.ingramcontent.com/pod-product-compliance
Lightning Source LLC
La Vergne TN
LVHW020711110826
845149LV00012B/2211

* 9 7 9 8 9 9 2 6 9 3 3 4 8 *